ARTHUR & LANCELOT
THE FIGHT FOR CAMELOT

A
BRITISH
LEGEND

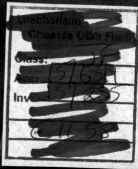

GRAPHIC UNIVERSE™

STORY BY
JEFF LIMKE
PENCILS AND INKS BY
THOMAS YEATES

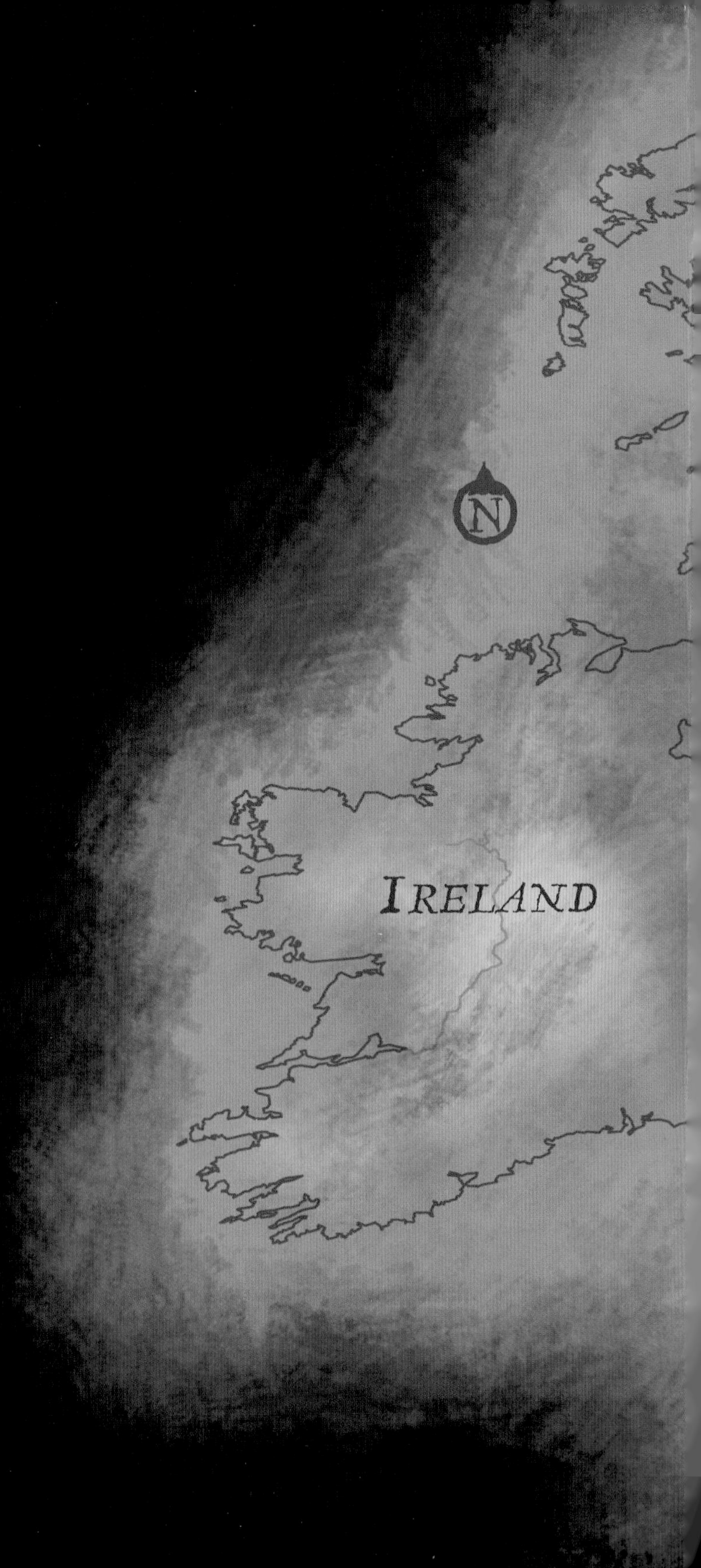
N
IRELAND

ARTHUR & LANCELOT

THE FIGHT FOR CAMELOT

A BRITISH LEGEND

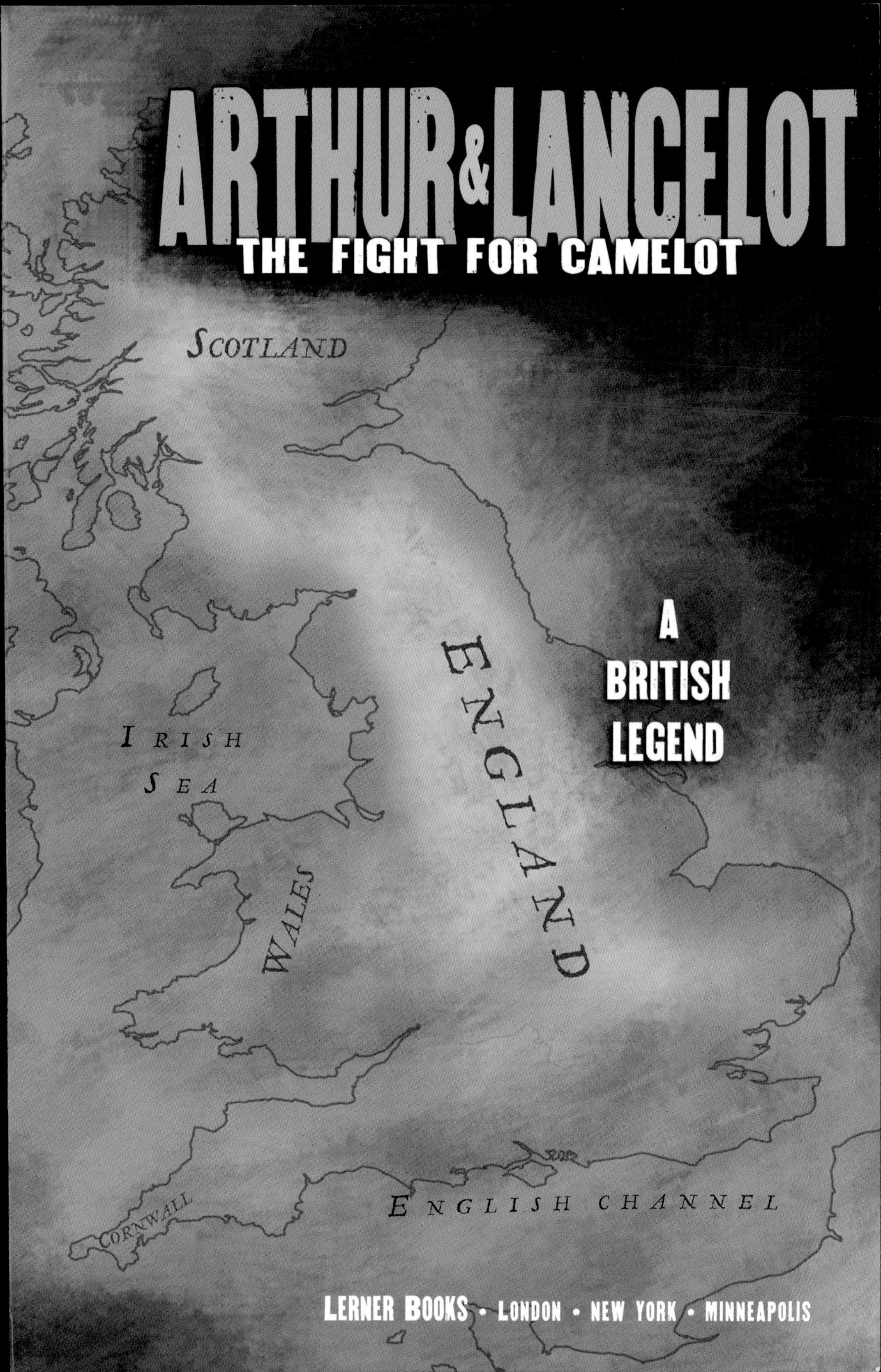
SCOTLAND
IRISH SEA
ENGLAND
WALES
CORNWALL
ENGLISH CHANNEL

LERNER BOOKS • LONDON • NEW YORK • MINNEAPOLIS

Whether King Arthur was a real person is unknown, but his story is set amid real events in British history. He would have lived around AD 400 or 500, when the many small kingdoms of Britain were fighting each other and against foreign invaders. Arthur is thus seen as the king who united and defended early Britain. But often Arthurian tales are depicted as taking place much later in the Middle Ages (about 1100–1300), with knights in armour, jousts and castles. **Arthur & Lancelot: The Fight for Camelot** follows that tradition.

As the story begins, Arthur has been king for many years. He rules from Camelot, where a wondrous castle serves as a symbol for the peace of the realm. Arthur leads the Knights of the Round Table, each chosen for his courage and loyalty. But even at Camelot, Arthur must beware those who want to steal his power. As this struggle draws in Arthur's wife, Guinevere, and his friend Lancelot, the king is faced with a conflict between his private feelings and his public duties.

Author Jeff Limke adapted this story from *Le Morte d'Arthur*, a fifteenth-century collection of Arthurian tales. Artist Thomas Yeates used historical and traditional sources for heraldry, costuming, armour and other visual details. Consultant Andrew Scheil ensured accuracy

STORY BY JEFF LIMKE

PENCILS AND INKS BY THOMAS YEATES
WITH SAM GLANZMAN AND KEN HOOPER

COLOURING BY HI–FI COLOUR DESIGN

LETTERING BY BRIAN CROWLEY

CONSULTANT: ANDREW SCHEIL, PHD, UNIVERSITY OF MINNESOTA

Graphic Universe™ is a trademark of Lerner Publishing Group, Inc.

First published in the United Kingdom in 2009 by Lerner Books,
Dalton House,
60 Windsor Avenue,
London SW19 2RR

Website address: www.lernerbooks.co.uk

This edition was updated and edited for UK publication by Discovery Books Ltd., First Floor, 2 College Street, Ludlow, Shropshire SY8 1AN

British Library Cataloguing in Publication Data

Limke, Jeff
    Arthur and Lancelot : the fight for Camelot. – 2nd ed. – (Graphic universe)
    1. Arthur, King – Comic books, strips, etc. – Juvenile fiction 2. Lancelot (Legendary character) – Comic books, strips, etc. – Juvenile fiction 3. Camelot (Legendary place) – Comic books, strips, etc. – Juvenile fiction 4. Children's stories – Comic books, strips, etc.
    I. Title II. Yeates, Thomas
    741.5

ISBN-13: 978 0 7613 4346 2

TABLE OF CONTENTS

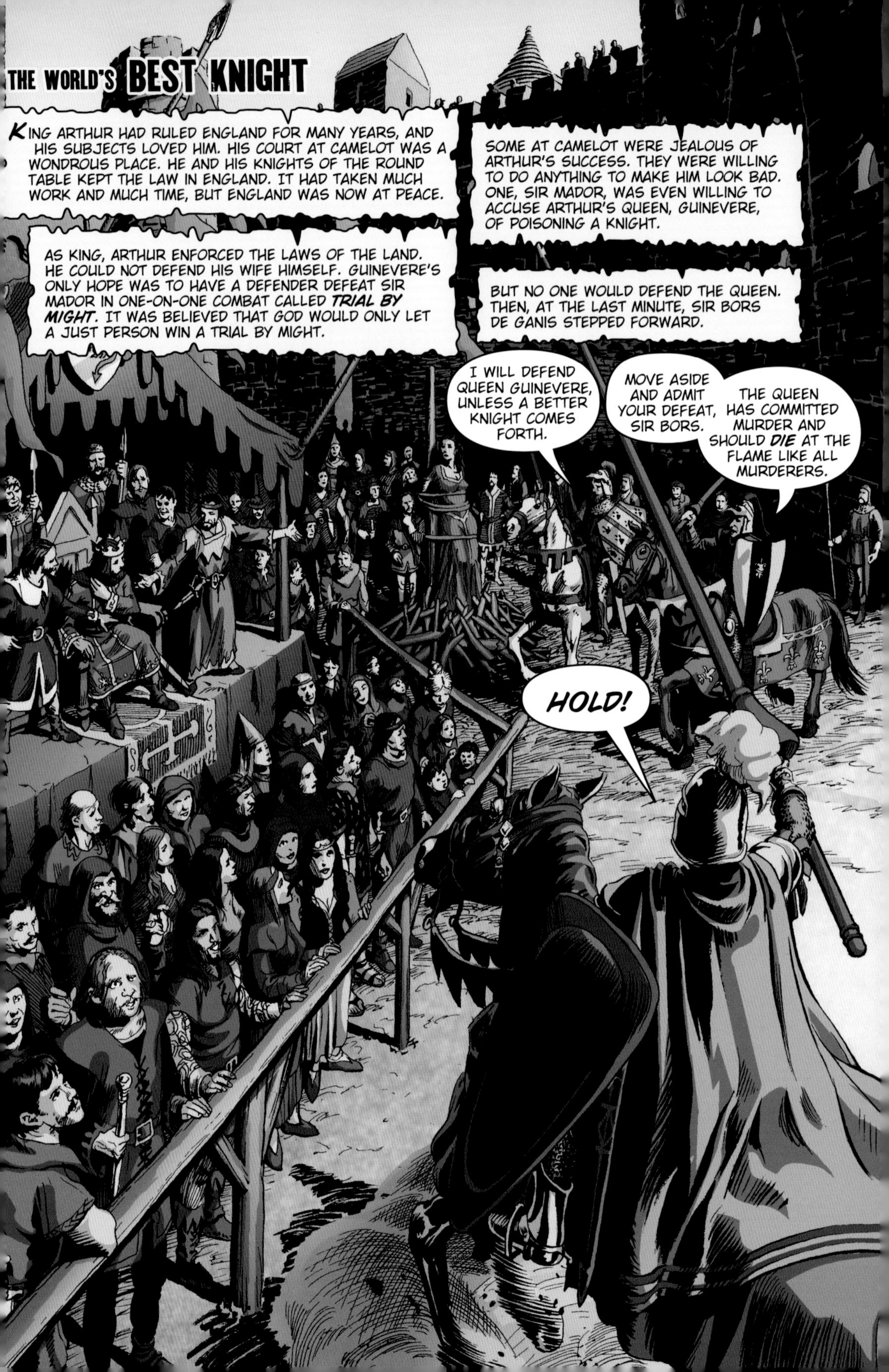
THE WORLD'S BEST KNIGHT
KING ARTHUR HAD RULED ENGLAND FOR MANY YEARS, AND HIS SUBJECTS LOVED HIM. HIS COURT AT CAMELOT WAS A WONDROUS PLACE. HE AND HIS KNIGHTS OF THE ROUND TABLE KEPT THE LAW IN ENGLAND. IT HAD TAKEN MUCH WORK AND MUCH TIME, BUT ENGLAND WAS NOW AT PEACE.
SOME AT CAMELOT WERE JEALOUS OF ARTHUR'S SUCCESS. THEY WERE WILLING TO DO ANYTHING TO MAKE HIM LOOK BAD. ONE, SIR MADOR, WAS EVEN WILLING TO ACCUSE ARTHUR'S QUEEN, GUINEVERE, OF POISONING A KNIGHT.
AS KING, ARTHUR ENFORCED THE LAWS OF THE LAND. HE COULD NOT DEFEND HIS WIFE HIMSELF. GUINEVERE'S ONLY HOPE WAS TO HAVE A DEFENDER DEFEAT SIR MADOR IN ONE-ON-ONE COMBAT CALLED ***TRIAL BY MIGHT***. IT WAS BELIEVED THAT GOD WOULD ONLY LET A JUST PERSON WIN A TRIAL BY MIGHT.
BUT NO ONE WOULD DEFEND THE QUEEN. THEN, AT THE LAST MINUTE, SIR BORS DE GANIS STEPPED FORWARD.
I WILL DEFEND QUEEN GUINEVERE, UNLESS A BETTER KNIGHT COMES FORTH.
MOVE ASIDE AND ADMIT YOUR DEFEAT, SIR BORS.
THE QUEEN HAS COMMITTED MURDER AND SHOULD ***DIE*** AT THE FLAME LIKE ALL MURDERERS.
HOLD!

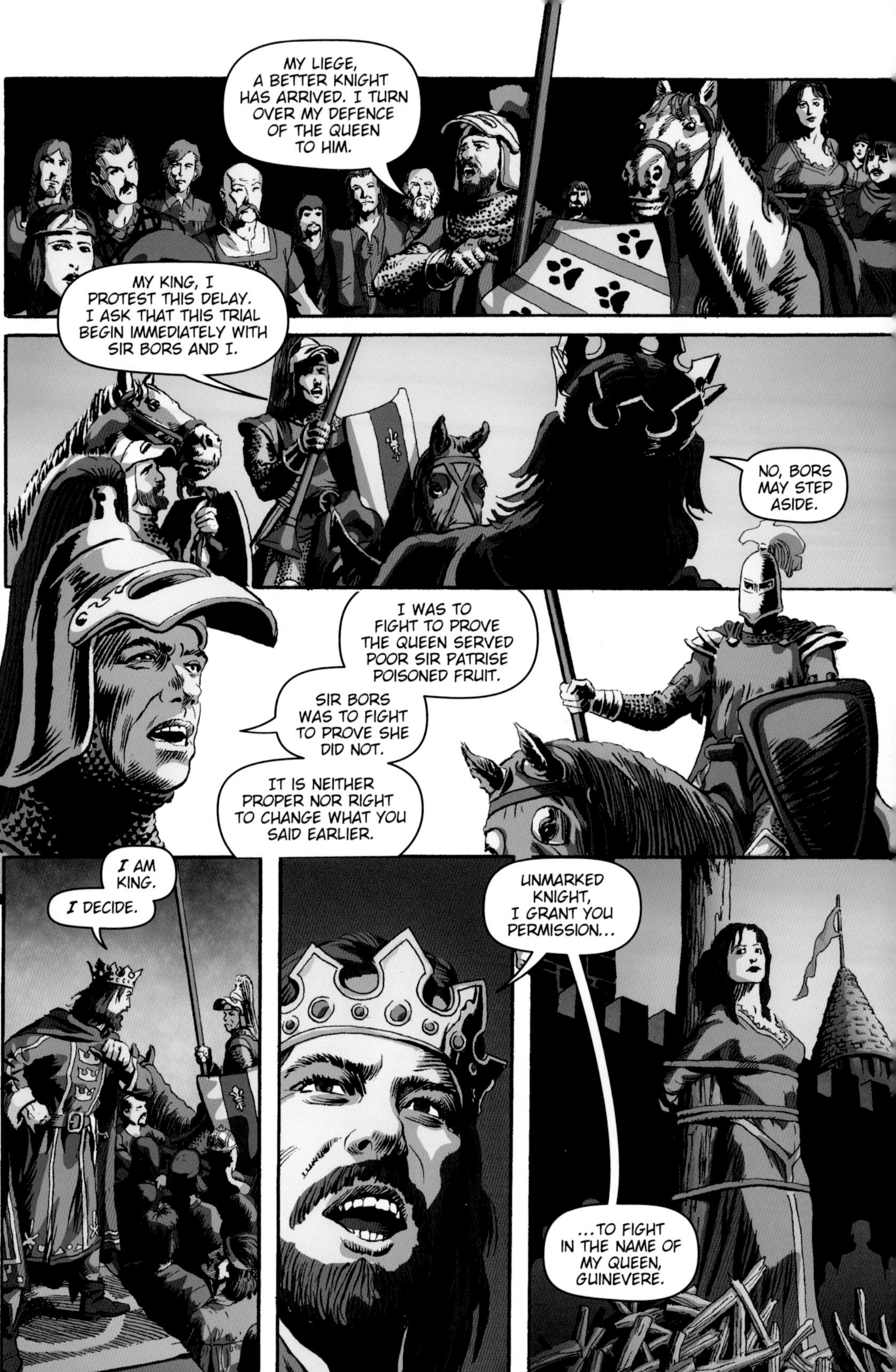
MY LIEGE, A BETTER KNIGHT HAS ARRIVED. I TURN OVER MY DEFENCE OF THE QUEEN TO HIM.
MY KING, I PROTEST THIS DELAY. I ASK THAT THIS TRIAL BEGIN IMMEDIATELY WITH SIR BORS AND I.
NO, BORS MAY STEP ASIDE.
I WAS TO FIGHT TO PROVE THE QUEEN SERVED POOR SIR PATRISE POISONED FRUIT.
SIR BORS WAS TO FIGHT TO PROVE SHE DID NOT.
IT IS NEITHER PROPER NOR RIGHT TO CHANGE WHAT YOU SAID EARLIER.
I AM KING.
I DECIDE.
UNMARKED KNIGHT, I GRANT YOU PERMISSION...
...TO FIGHT IN THE NAME OF MY QUEEN, GUINEVERE.

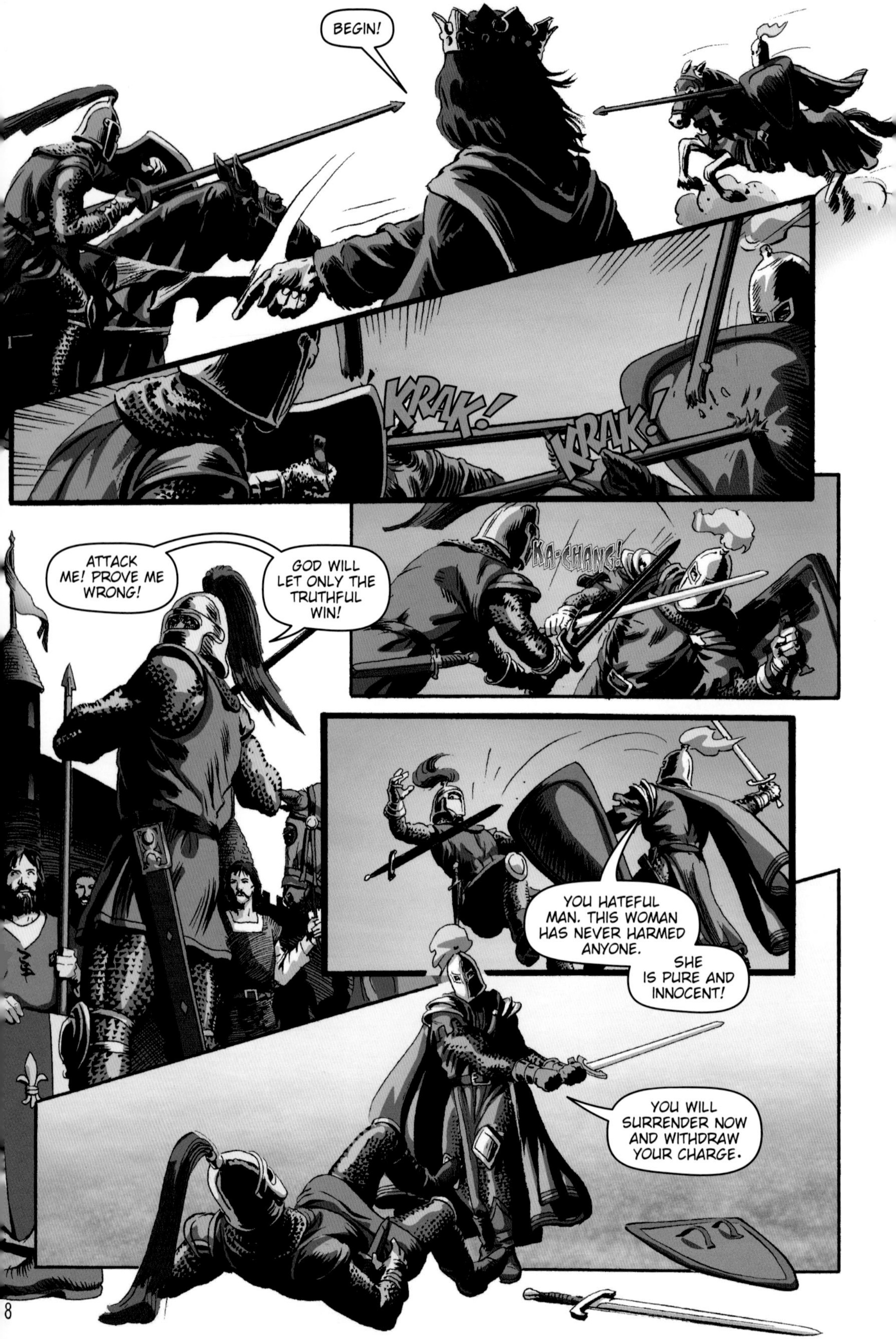
BEGIN!
KRAK!
KRAK!
KA-CHANG!
ATTACK ME! PROVE ME WRONG!
GOD WILL LET ONLY THE TRUTHFUL WIN!
YOU HATEFUL MAN. THIS WOMAN HAS NEVER HARMED ANYONE.
SHE IS PURE AND INNOCENT!
YOU WILL SURRENDER NOW AND WITHDRAW YOUR CHARGE.

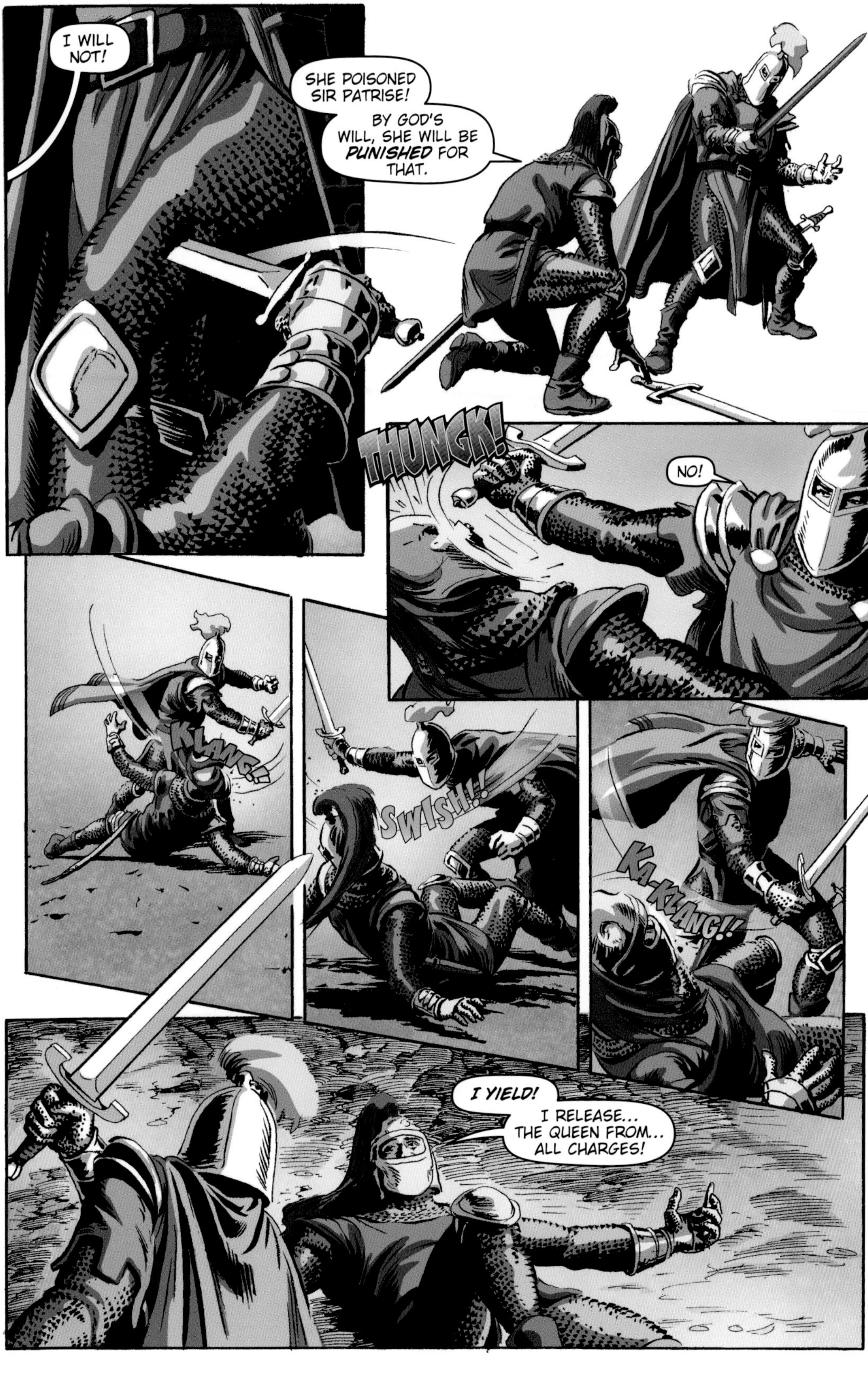
I WILL NOT!
SHE POISONED SIR PATRISE!
BY GOD'S WILL, SHE WILL BE PUNISHED FOR THAT.
THUNGK!
NO!
KLANG!!
SWISH!!
KA-KLANG!!
I YIELD!
I RELEASE... THE QUEEN FROM... ALL CHARGES!

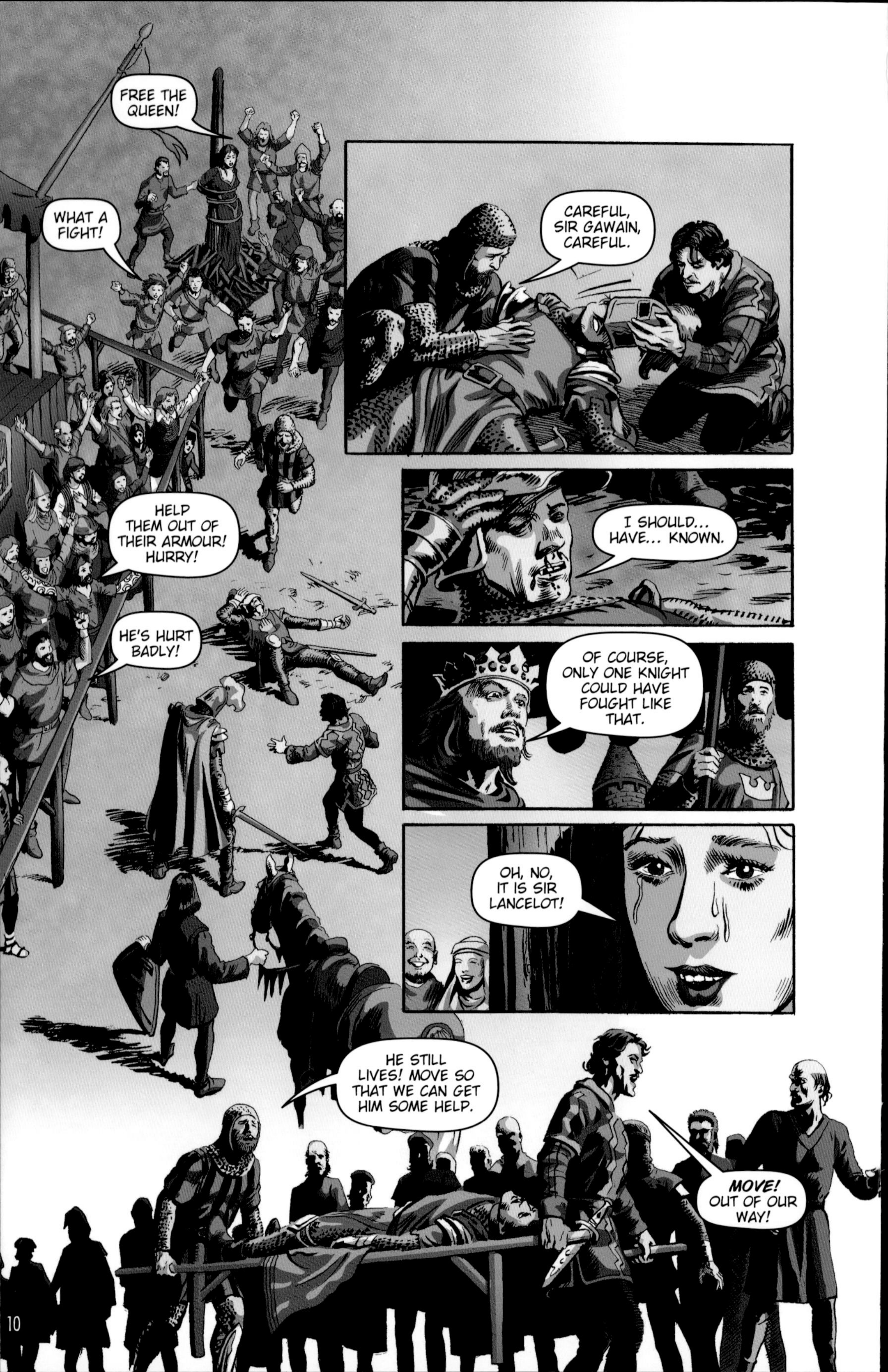
FREE THE QUEEN!
WHAT A FIGHT!
HELP THEM OUT OF THEIR ARMOUR! HURRY!
HE'S HURT BADLY!
CAREFUL, SIR GAWAIN, CAREFUL.
I SHOULD... HAVE... KNOWN.
OF COURSE, ONLY ONE KNIGHT COULD HAVE FOUGHT LIKE THAT.
OH, NO, IT IS SIR LANCELOT!
HE STILL LIVES! MOVE SO THAT WE CAN GET HIM SOME HELP.
MOVE! OUT OF OUR WAY!

THE WINCHESTER TOURNAMENT

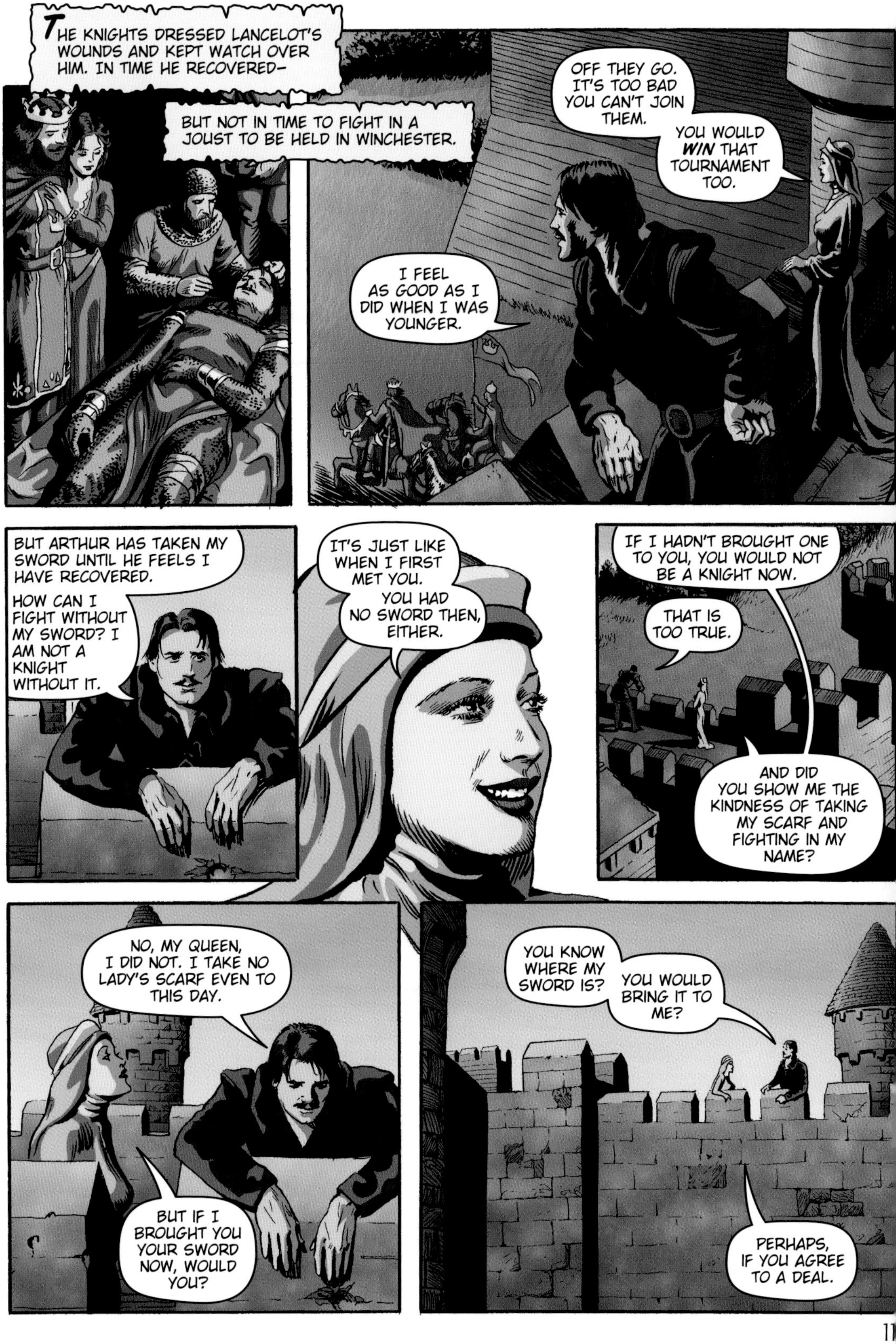
THE KNIGHTS DRESSED LANCELOT'S WOUNDS AND KEPT WATCH OVER HIM. IN TIME HE RECOVERED–
BUT NOT IN TIME TO FIGHT IN A JOUST TO BE HELD IN WINCHESTER.
OFF THEY GO. IT'S TOO BAD YOU CAN'T JOIN THEM.
YOU WOULD WIN THAT TOURNAMENT TOO.
I FEEL AS GOOD AS I DID WHEN I WAS YOUNGER.
BUT ARTHUR HAS TAKEN MY SWORD UNTIL HE FEELS I HAVE RECOVERED.
HOW CAN I FIGHT WITHOUT MY SWORD? I AM NOT A KNIGHT WITHOUT IT.
IT'S JUST LIKE WHEN I FIRST MET YOU.
YOU HAD NO SWORD THEN, EITHER.
IF I HADN'T BROUGHT ONE TO YOU, YOU WOULD NOT BE A KNIGHT NOW.
THAT IS TOO TRUE.
AND DID YOU SHOW ME THE KINDNESS OF TAKING MY SCARF AND FIGHTING IN MY NAME?
NO, MY QUEEN, I DID NOT. I TAKE NO LADY'S SCARF EVEN TO THIS DAY.
BUT IF I BROUGHT YOU YOUR SWORD NOW, WOULD YOU?
YOU KNOW WHERE MY SWORD IS?
YOU WOULD BRING IT TO ME?
PERHAPS, IF YOU AGREE TO A DEAL.

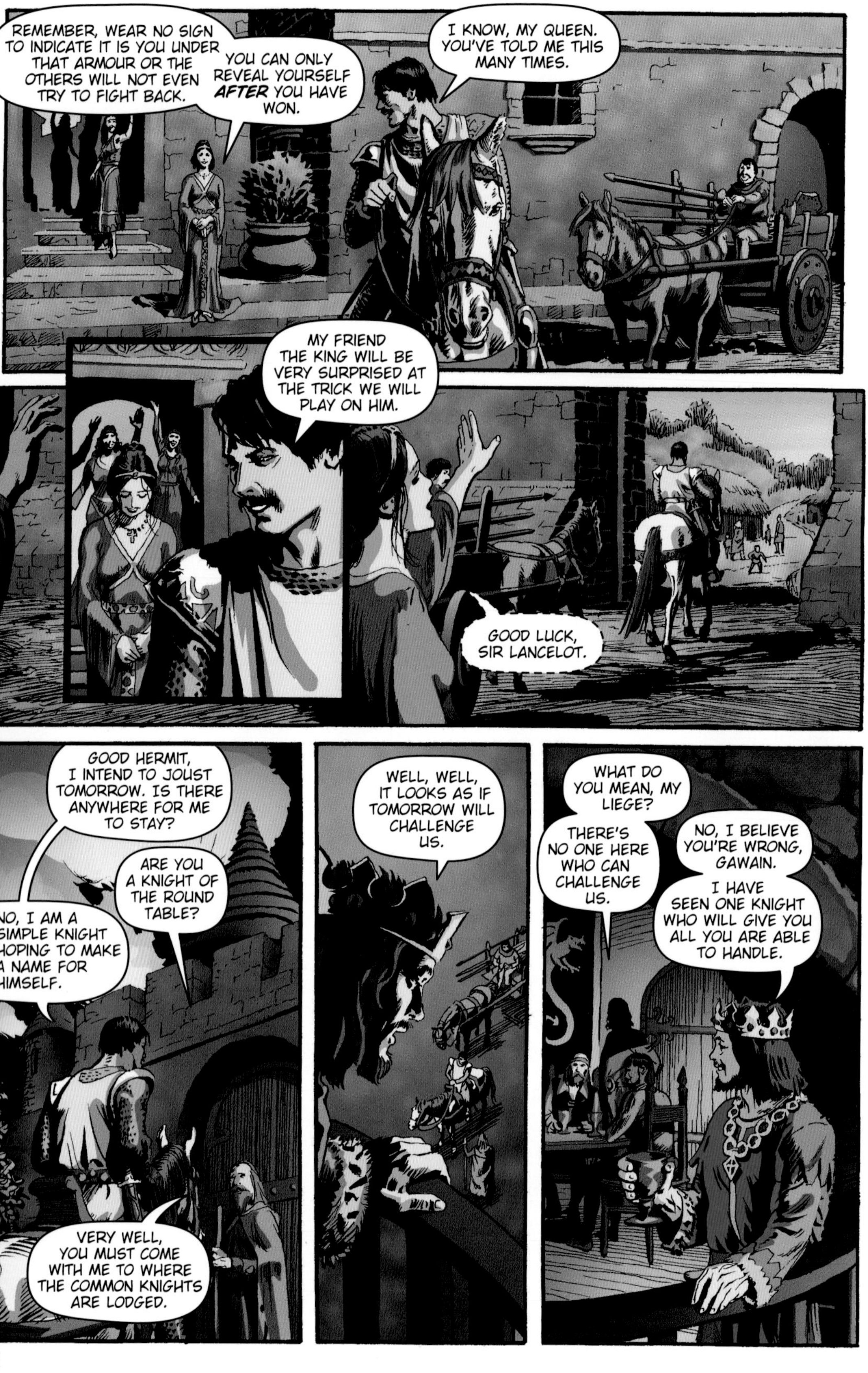
REMEMBER, WEAR NO SIGN TO INDICATE IT IS YOU UNDER THAT ARMOUR OR THE OTHERS WILL NOT EVEN TRY TO FIGHT BACK.
YOU CAN ONLY REVEAL YOURSELF *AFTER* YOU HAVE WON.
I KNOW, MY QUEEN. YOU'VE TOLD ME THIS MANY TIMES.
MY FRIEND THE KING WILL BE VERY SURPRISED AT THE TRICK WE WILL PLAY ON HIM.
GOOD LUCK, SIR LANCELOT.
GOOD HERMIT, I INTEND TO JOUST TOMORROW. IS THERE ANYWHERE FOR ME TO STAY?
ARE YOU A KNIGHT OF THE ROUND TABLE?
NO, I AM A SIMPLE KNIGHT HOPING TO MAKE A NAME FOR HIMSELF.
VERY WELL, YOU MUST COME WITH ME TO WHERE THE COMMON KNIGHTS ARE LODGED.
WELL, WELL, IT LOOKS AS IF TOMORROW WILL CHALLENGE US.
WHAT DO YOU MEAN, MY LIEGE?
THERE'S NO ONE HERE WHO CAN CHALLENGE US.
NO, I BELIEVE YOU'RE WRONG, GAWAIN.
I HAVE SEEN ONE KNIGHT WHO WILL GIVE YOU ALL YOU ARE ABLE TO HANDLE.

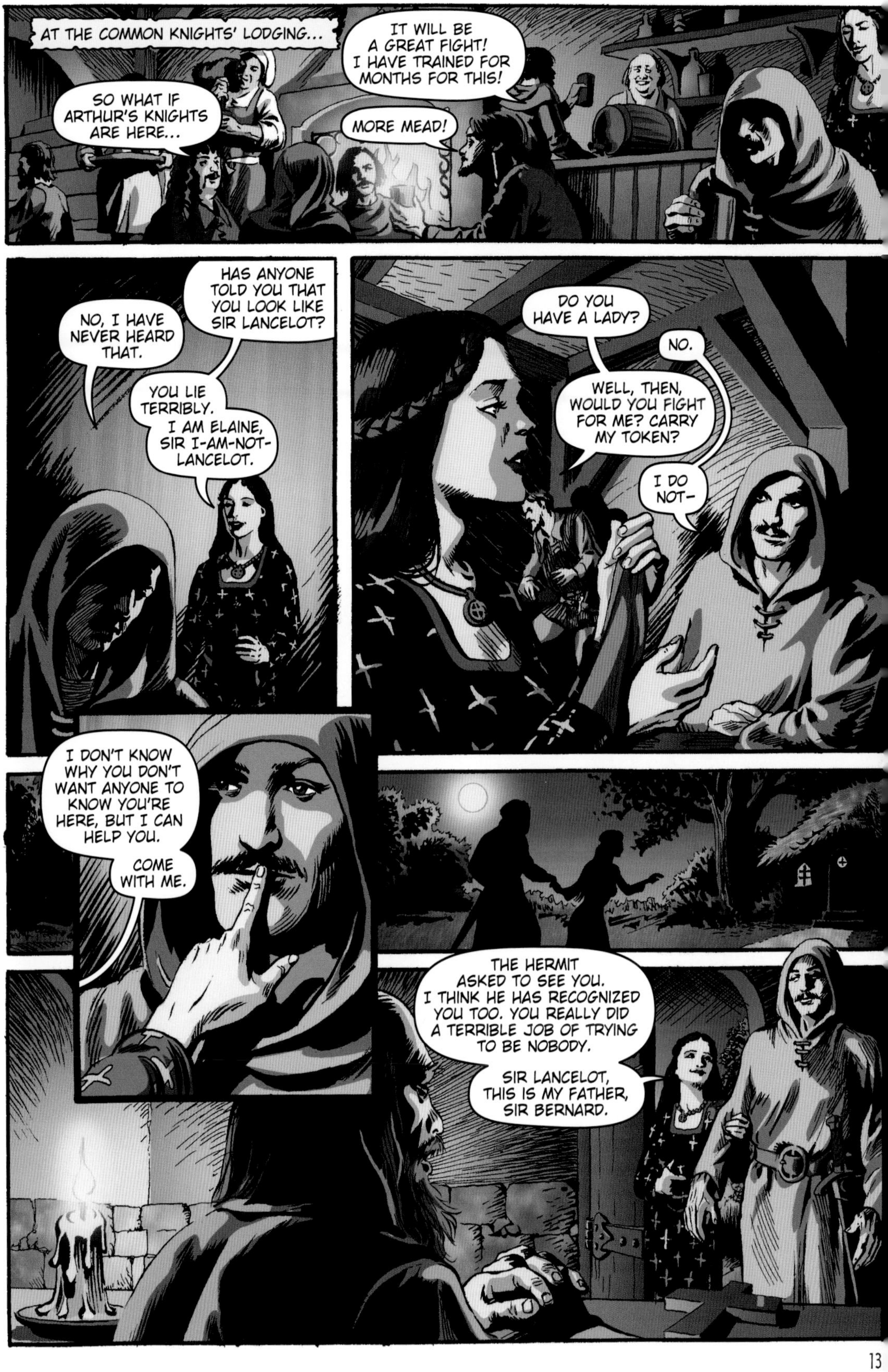

AT THE COMMON KNIGHTS' LODGING...
SO WHAT IF ARTHUR'S KNIGHTS ARE HERE...
IT WILL BE A GREAT FIGHT! I HAVE TRAINED FOR MONTHS FOR THIS!
MORE MEAD!
HAS ANYONE TOLD YOU THAT YOU LOOK LIKE SIR LANCELOT?
NO, I HAVE NEVER HEARD THAT.
YOU LIE TERRIBLY.
I AM ELAINE, SIR I-AM-NOT-LANCELOT.
DO YOU HAVE A LADY?
NO.
WELL, THEN, WOULD YOU FIGHT FOR ME? CARRY MY TOKEN?
I DO NOT-
I DON'T KNOW WHY YOU DON'T WANT ANYONE TO KNOW YOU'RE HERE, BUT I CAN HELP YOU.
COME WITH ME.
THE HERMIT ASKED TO SEE YOU. I THINK HE HAS RECOGNIZED YOU TOO. YOU REALLY DID A TERRIBLE JOB OF TRYING TO BE NOBODY.
SIR LANCELOT, THIS IS MY FATHER, SIR BERNARD.

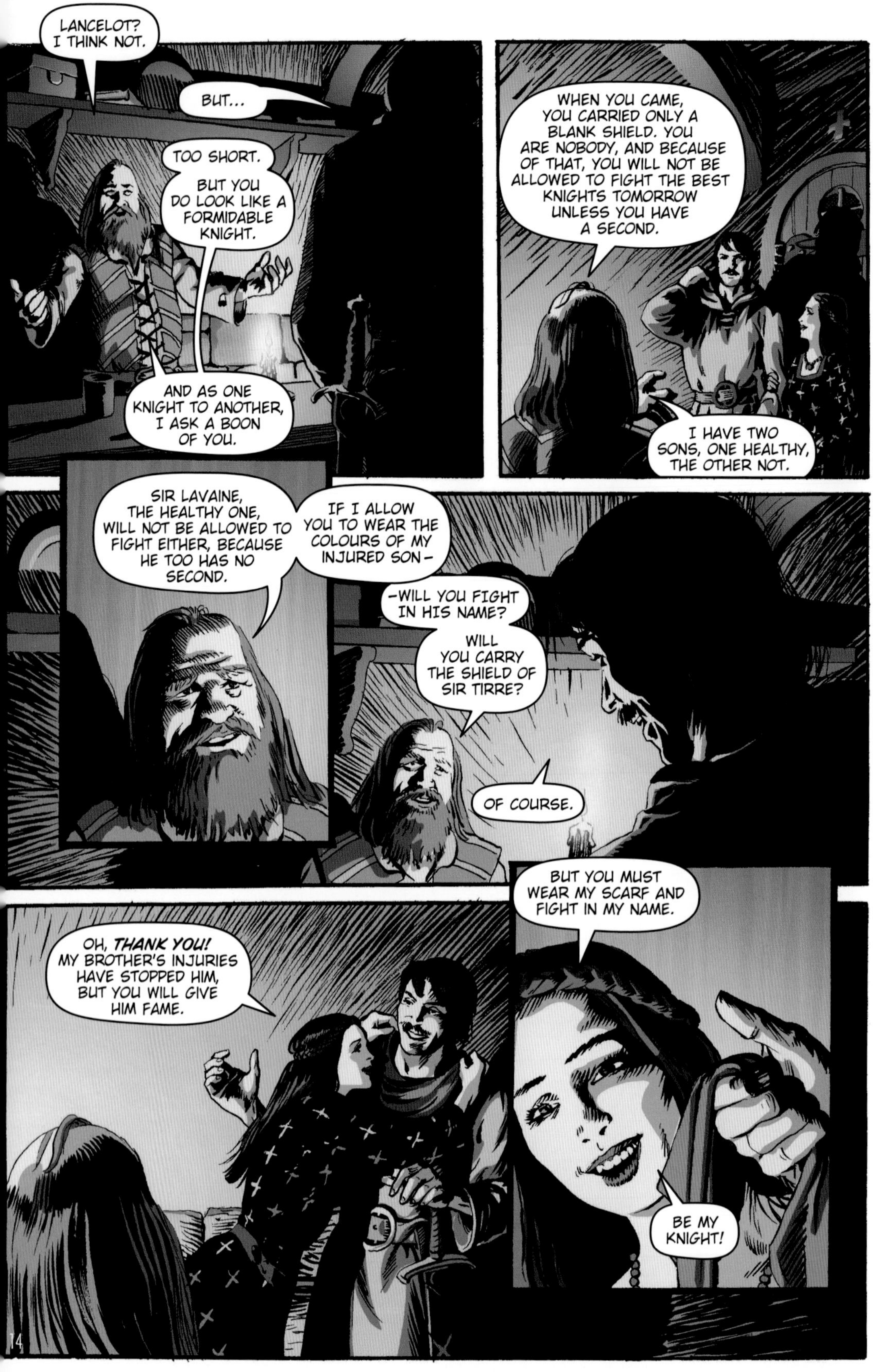

LANCELOT? I THINK NOT.
BUT...
TOO SHORT.
BUT YOU DO LOOK LIKE A FORMIDABLE KNIGHT.
AND AS ONE KNIGHT TO ANOTHER, I ASK A BOON OF YOU.
WHEN YOU CAME, YOU CARRIED ONLY A BLANK SHIELD. YOU ARE NOBODY, AND BECAUSE OF THAT, YOU WILL NOT BE ALLOWED TO FIGHT THE BEST KNIGHTS TOMORROW UNLESS YOU HAVE A SECOND.
I HAVE TWO SONS, ONE HEALTHY, THE OTHER NOT.
SIR LAVAINE, THE HEALTHY ONE, WILL NOT BE ALLOWED TO FIGHT EITHER, BECAUSE HE TOO HAS NO SECOND.
IF I ALLOW YOU TO WEAR THE COLOURS OF MY INJURED SON—
—WILL YOU FIGHT IN HIS NAME?
WILL YOU CARRY THE SHIELD OF SIR TIRRE?
OF COURSE.
OH, ***THANK YOU!*** MY BROTHER'S INJURIES HAVE STOPPED HIM, BUT YOU WILL GIVE HIM FAME.
BUT YOU MUST WEAR MY SCARF AND FIGHT IN MY NAME.
BE MY KNIGHT!

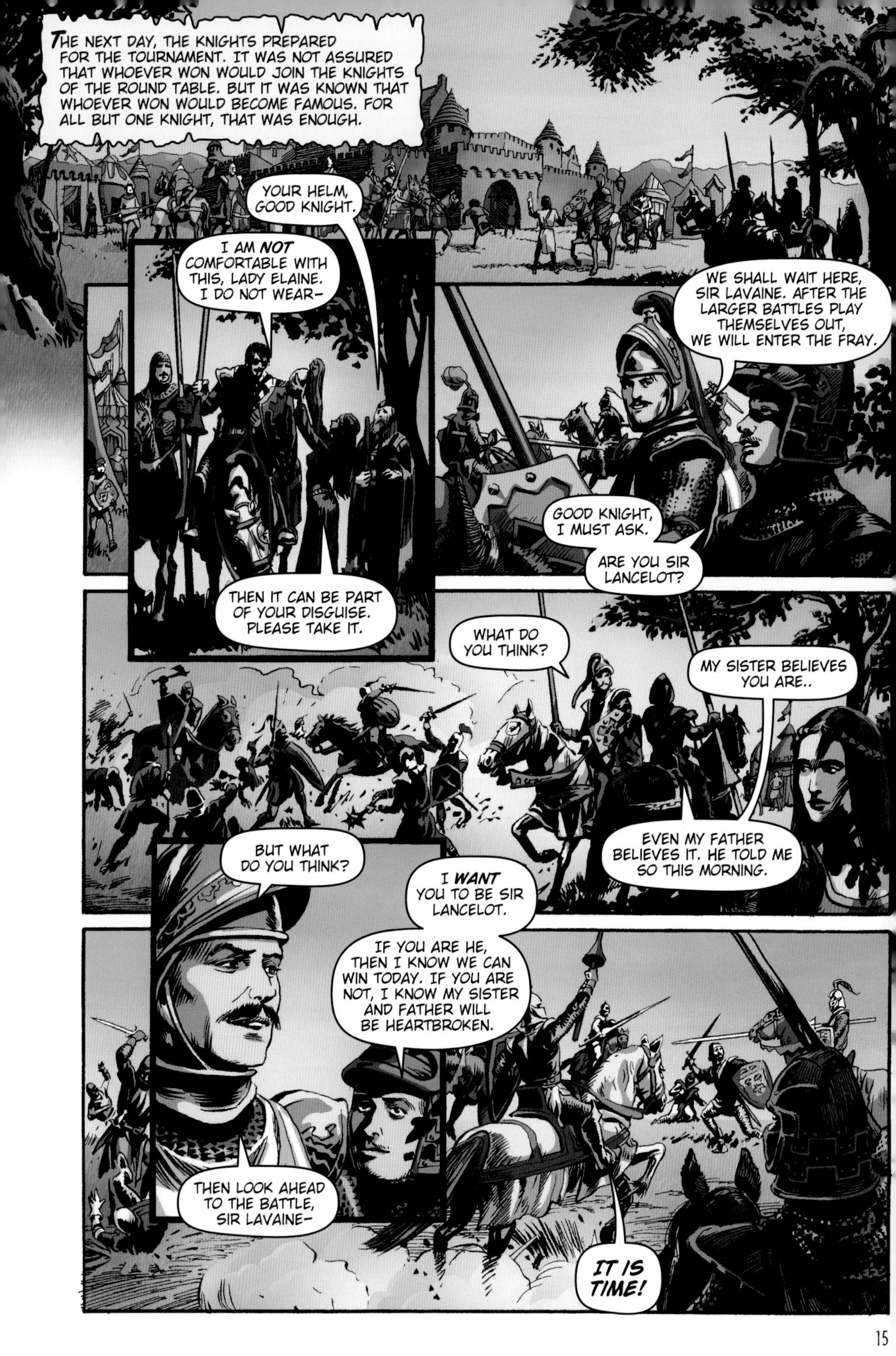
THE NEXT DAY, THE KNIGHTS PREPARED FOR THE TOURNAMENT. IT WAS NOT ASSURED THAT WHOEVER WON WOULD JOIN THE KNIGHTS OF THE ROUND TABLE. BUT IT WAS KNOWN THAT WHOEVER WON WOULD BECOME FAMOUS. FOR ALL BUT ONE KNIGHT, THAT WAS ENOUGH.
YOUR HELM, GOOD KNIGHT.
I AM NOT COMFORTABLE WITH THIS, LADY ELAINE. I DO NOT WEAR-
THEN IT CAN BE PART OF YOUR DISGUISE. PLEASE TAKE IT.
WE SHALL WAIT HERE, SIR LAVAINE. AFTER THE LARGER BATTLES PLAY THEMSELVES OUT, WE WILL ENTER THE FRAY.
GOOD KNIGHT, I MUST ASK.
ARE YOU SIR LANCELOT?
WHAT DO YOU THINK?
MY SISTER BELIEVES YOU ARE..
EVEN MY FATHER BELIEVES IT. HE TOLD ME SO THIS MORNING.
BUT WHAT DO YOU THINK?
I WANT YOU TO BE SIR LANCELOT.
IF YOU ARE HE, THEN I KNOW WE CAN WIN TODAY. IF YOU ARE NOT, I KNOW MY SISTER AND FATHER WILL BE HEARTBROKEN.
THEN LOOK AHEAD TO THE BATTLE, SIR LAVAINE-
IT IS TIME!

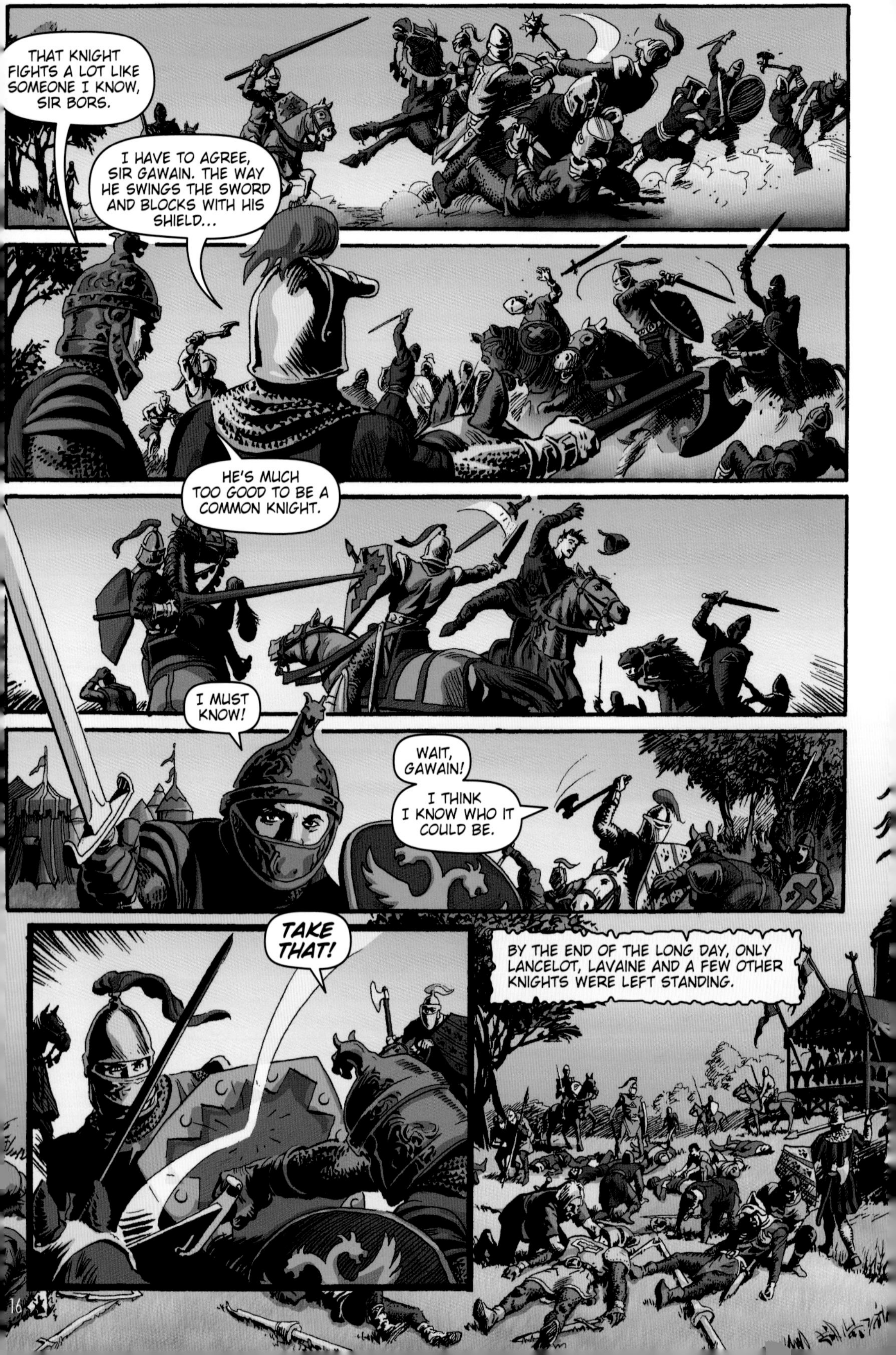

THAT KNIGHT FIGHTS A LOT LIKE SOMEONE I KNOW, SIR BORS.
I HAVE TO AGREE, SIR GAWAIN. THE WAY HE SWINGS THE SWORD AND BLOCKS WITH HIS SHIELD...
HE'S MUCH TOO GOOD TO BE A COMMON KNIGHT.
I MUST KNOW!
WAIT, GAWAIN!
I THINK I KNOW WHO IT COULD BE.
TAKE THAT!
BY THE END OF THE LONG DAY, ONLY LANCELOT, LAVAINE AND A FEW OTHER KNIGHTS WERE LEFT STANDING.

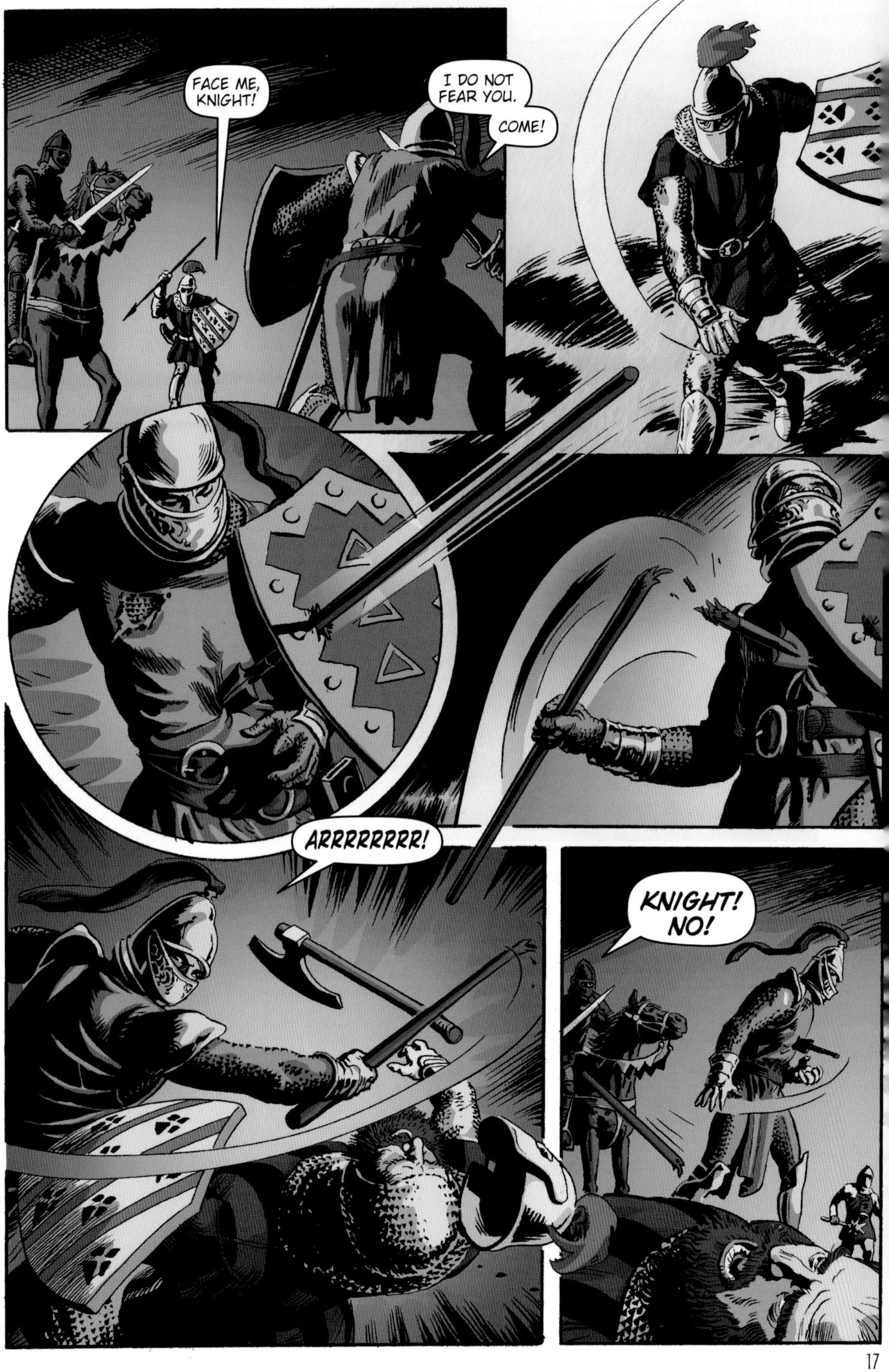
FACE ME, KNIGHT!
I DO NOT FEAR YOU.
COME!
ARRRRRRRR!
KNIGHT! NO!

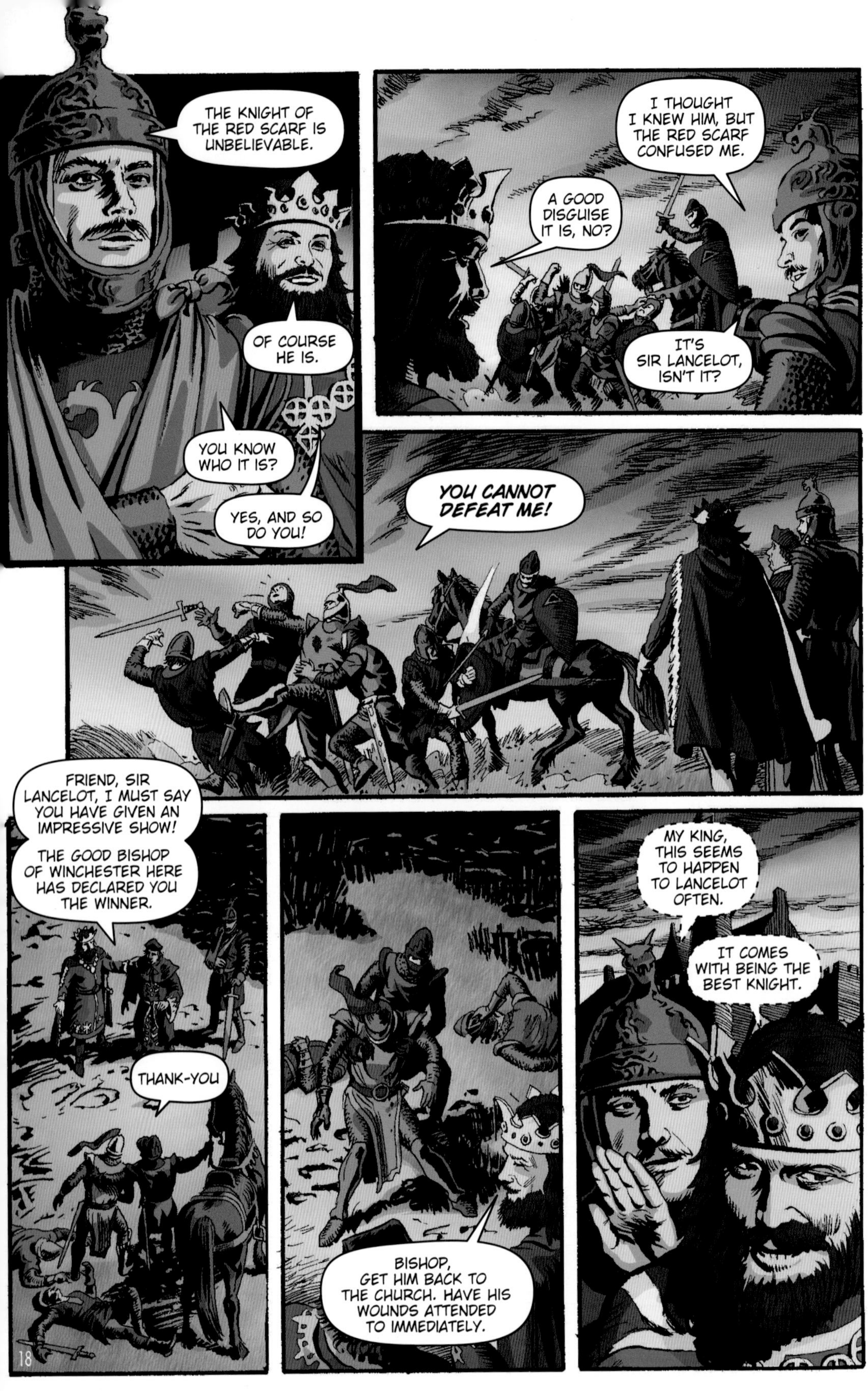
THE KNIGHT OF THE RED SCARF IS UNBELIEVABLE.
OF COURSE HE IS.
YOU KNOW WHO IT IS?
YES, AND SO DO YOU!
I THOUGHT I KNEW HIM, BUT THE RED SCARF CONFUSED ME.
A GOOD DISGUISE IT IS, NO?
IT'S SIR LANCELOT, ISN'T IT?
YOU CANNOT DEFEAT ME!
FRIEND, SIR LANCELOT, I MUST SAY YOU HAVE GIVEN AN IMPRESSIVE SHOW!
THE GOOD BISHOP OF WINCHESTER HERE HAS DECLARED YOU THE WINNER.
THANK-YOU
BISHOP, GET HIM BACK TO THE CHURCH. HAVE HIS WOUNDS ATTENDED TO IMMEDIATELY.
MY KING, THIS SEEMS TO HAPPEN TO LANCELOT OFTEN.
IT COMES WITH BEING THE BEST KNIGHT.

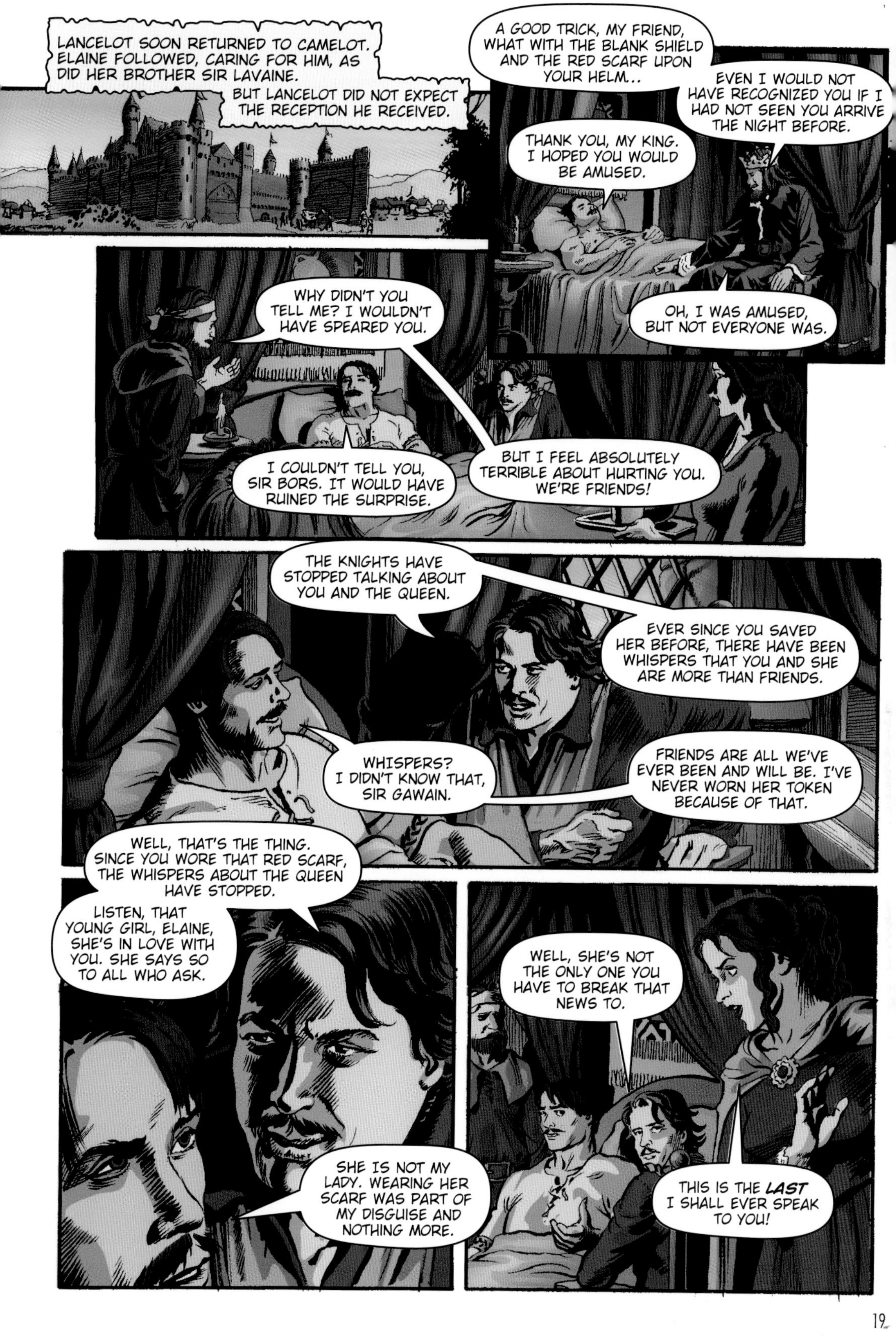
LANCELOT SOON RETURNED TO CAMELOT. ELAINE FOLLOWED, CARING FOR HIM, AS DID HER BROTHER SIR LAVAINE.
BUT LANCELOT DID NOT EXPECT THE RECEPTION HE RECEIVED.
A GOOD TRICK, MY FRIEND, WHAT WITH THE BLANK SHIELD AND THE RED SCARF UPON YOUR HELM...
EVEN I WOULD NOT HAVE RECOGNIZED YOU IF I HAD NOT SEEN YOU ARRIVE THE NIGHT BEFORE.
THANK YOU, MY KING. I HOPED YOU WOULD BE AMUSED.
OH, I WAS AMUSED, BUT NOT EVERYONE WAS.
WHY DIDN'T YOU TELL ME? I WOULDN'T HAVE SPEARED YOU.
I COULDN'T TELL YOU, SIR BORS. IT WOULD HAVE RUINED THE SURPRISE.
BUT I FEEL ABSOLUTELY TERRIBLE ABOUT HURTING YOU. WE'RE FRIENDS!
THE KNIGHTS HAVE STOPPED TALKING ABOUT YOU AND THE QUEEN.
EVER SINCE YOU SAVED HER BEFORE, THERE HAVE BEEN WHISPERS THAT YOU AND SHE ARE MORE THAN FRIENDS.
WHISPERS? I DIDN'T KNOW THAT, SIR GAWAIN.
FRIENDS ARE ALL WE'VE EVER BEEN AND WILL BE. I'VE NEVER WORN HER TOKEN BECAUSE OF THAT.
WELL, THAT'S THE THING. SINCE YOU WORE THAT RED SCARF, THE WHISPERS ABOUT THE QUEEN HAVE STOPPED.
LISTEN, THAT YOUNG GIRL, ELAINE, SHE'S IN LOVE WITH YOU. SHE SAYS SO TO ALL WHO ASK.
SHE IS NOT MY LADY. WEARING HER SCARF WAS PART OF MY DISGUISE AND NOTHING MORE.
WELL, SHE'S NOT THE ONLY ONE YOU HAVE TO BREAK THAT NEWS TO.
THIS IS THE ***LAST*** I SHALL EVER SPEAK TO YOU!

FOUL SIR MELIGRANCE

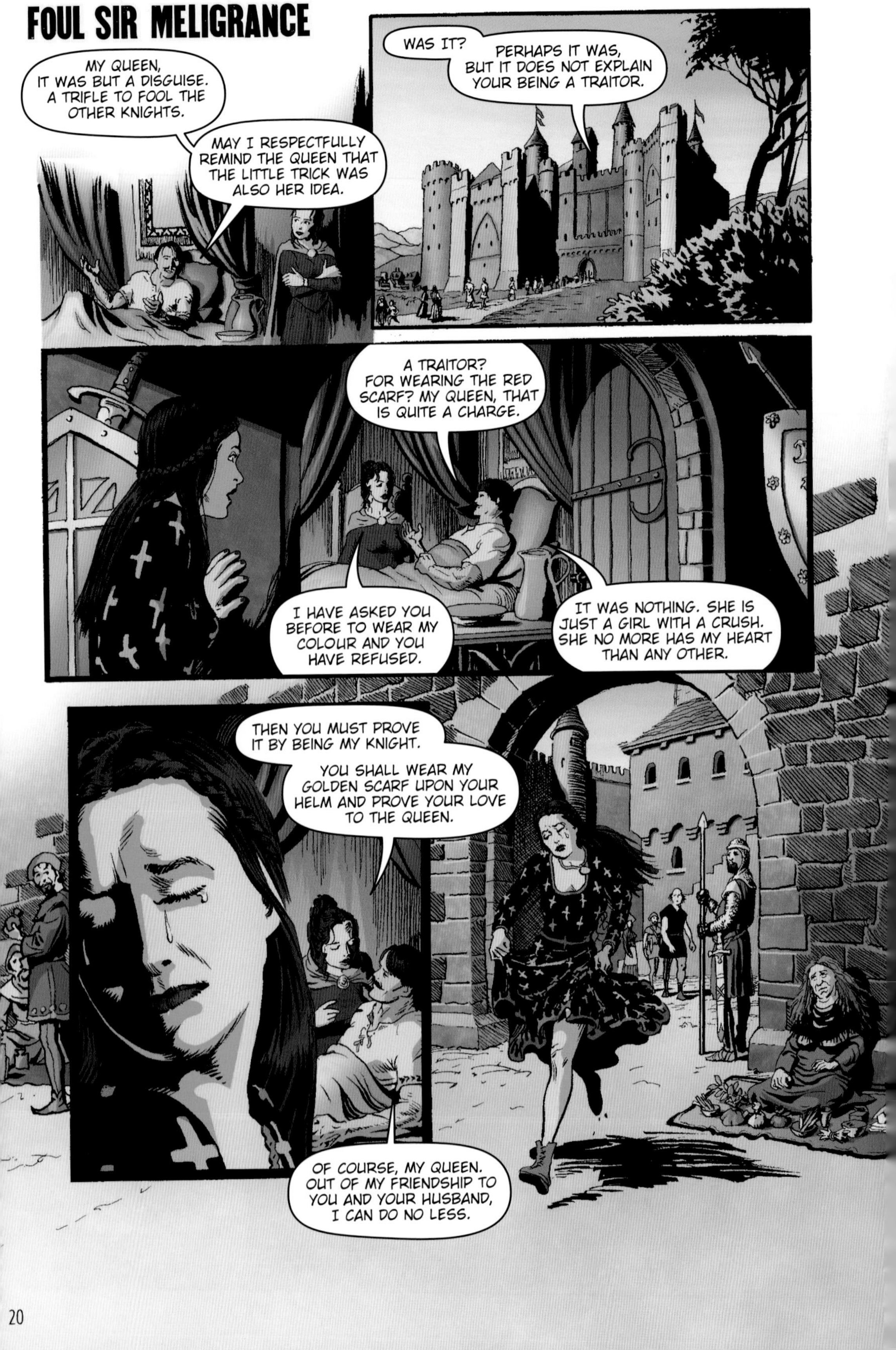
MY QUEEN, IT WAS BUT A DISGUISE. A TRIFLE TO FOOL THE OTHER KNIGHTS.
MAY I RESPECTFULLY REMIND THE QUEEN THAT THE LITTLE TRICK WAS ALSO HER IDEA.
WAS IT?
PERHAPS IT WAS, BUT IT DOES NOT EXPLAIN YOUR BEING A TRAITOR.
A TRAITOR? FOR WEARING THE RED SCARF? MY QUEEN, THAT IS QUITE A CHARGE.
I HAVE ASKED YOU BEFORE TO WEAR MY COLOUR AND YOU HAVE REFUSED.
IT WAS NOTHING. SHE IS JUST A GIRL WITH A CRUSH. SHE NO MORE HAS MY HEART THAN ANY OTHER.
THEN YOU MUST PROVE IT BY BEING MY KNIGHT.
YOU SHALL WEAR MY GOLDEN SCARF UPON YOUR HELM AND PROVE YOUR LOVE TO THE QUEEN.
OF COURSE, MY QUEEN. OUT OF MY FRIENDSHIP TO YOU AND YOUR HUSBAND, I CAN DO NO LESS.

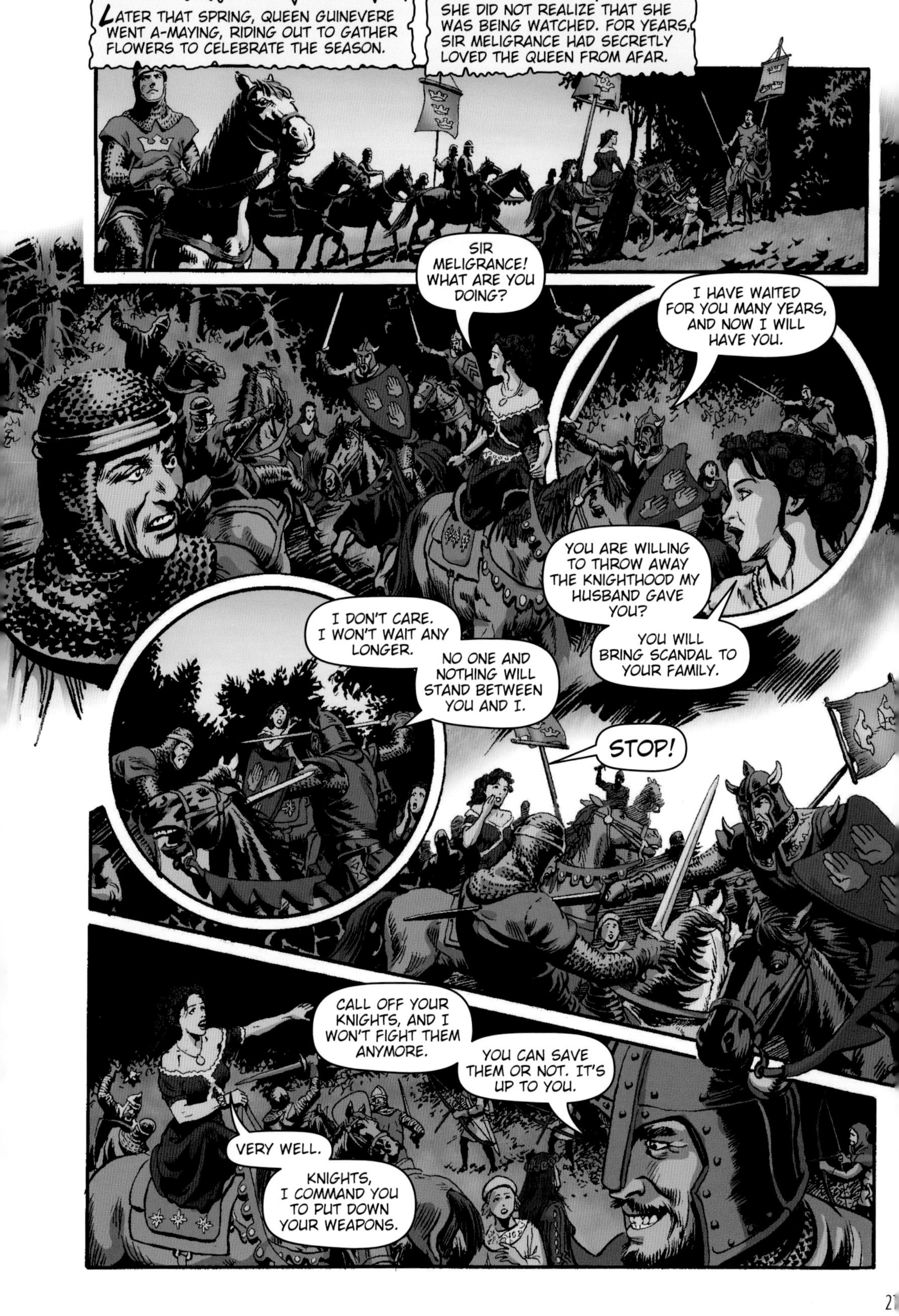
LATER THAT SPRING, QUEEN GUINEVERE WENT A-MAYING, RIDING OUT TO GATHER FLOWERS TO CELEBRATE THE SEASON.
SHE DID NOT REALIZE THAT SHE WAS BEING WATCHED. FOR YEARS, SIR MELIGRANCE HAD SECRETLY LOVED THE QUEEN FROM AFAR.
SIR MELIGRANCE! WHAT ARE YOU DOING?
I HAVE WAITED FOR YOU MANY YEARS, AND NOW I WILL HAVE YOU.
YOU ARE WILLING TO THROW AWAY THE KNIGHTHOOD MY HUSBAND GAVE YOU?
YOU WILL BRING SCANDAL TO YOUR FAMILY.
I DON'T CARE. I WON'T WAIT ANY LONGER.
NO ONE AND NOTHING WILL STAND BETWEEN YOU AND I.
STOP!
CALL OFF YOUR KNIGHTS, AND I WON'T FIGHT THEM ANYMORE.
YOU CAN SAVE THEM OR NOT. IT'S UP TO YOU.
VERY WELL.
KNIGHTS, I COMMAND YOU TO PUT DOWN YOUR WEAPONS.

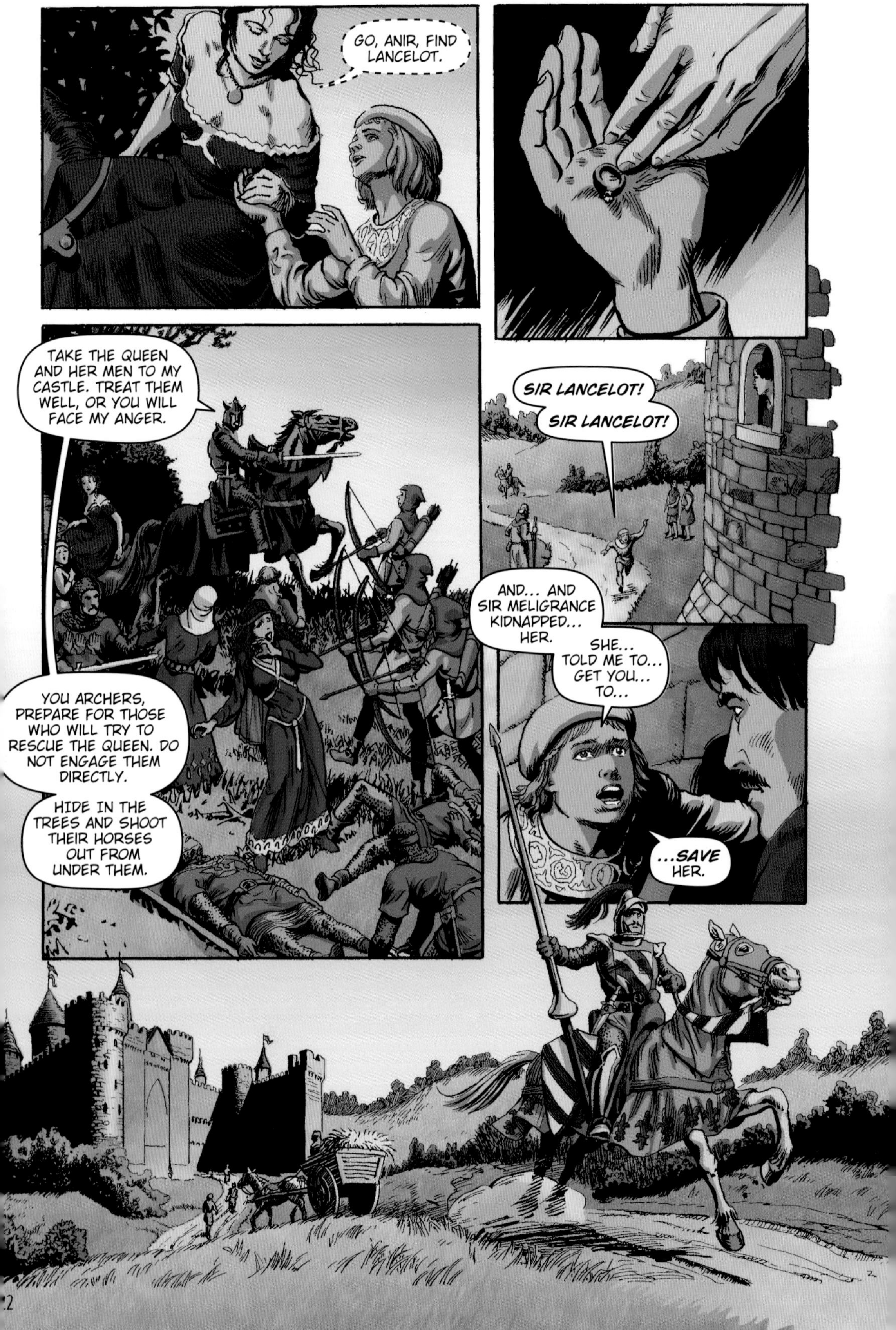
GO, ANIR, FIND LANCELOT.
TAKE THE QUEEN AND HER MEN TO MY CASTLE. TREAT THEM WELL, OR YOU WILL FACE MY ANGER.
YOU ARCHERS, PREPARE FOR THOSE WHO WILL TRY TO RESCUE THE QUEEN. DO NOT ENGAGE THEM DIRECTLY.
HIDE IN THE TREES AND SHOOT THEIR HORSES OUT FROM UNDER THEM.
SIR LANCELOT!
SIR LANCELOT!
AND... AND SIR MELIGRANCE KIDNAPPED... HER.
SHE... TOLD ME TO... GET YOU... TO...
...SAVE HER.

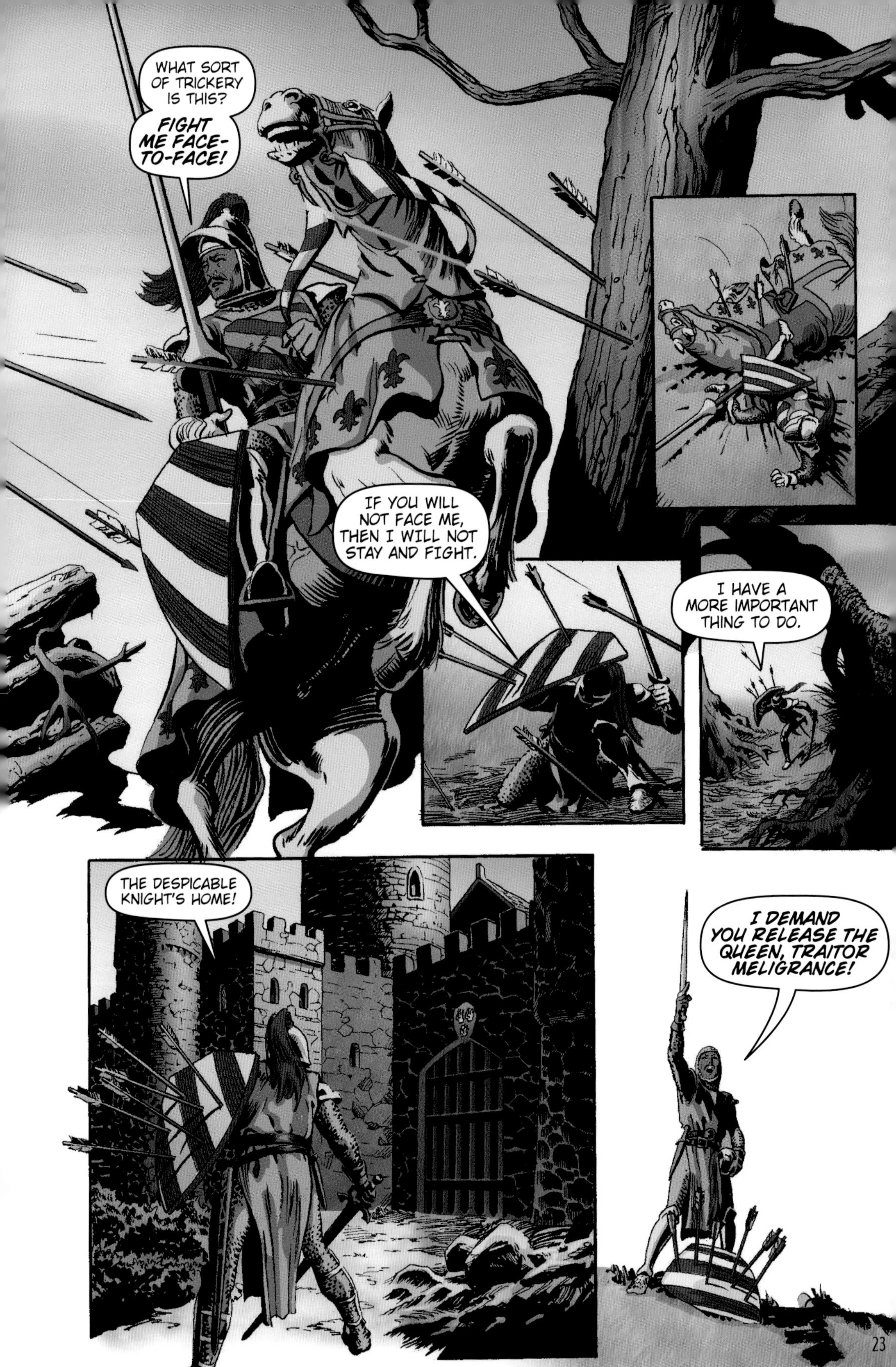
WHAT SORT OF TRICKERY IS THIS?
FIGHT ME FACE-TO-FACE!
IF YOU WILL NOT FACE ME, THEN I WILL NOT STAY AND FIGHT.
I HAVE A MORE IMPORTANT THING TO DO.
THE DESPICABLE KNIGHT'S HOME!
I DEMAND YOU RELEASE THE QUEEN, TRAITOR MELIGRANCE!

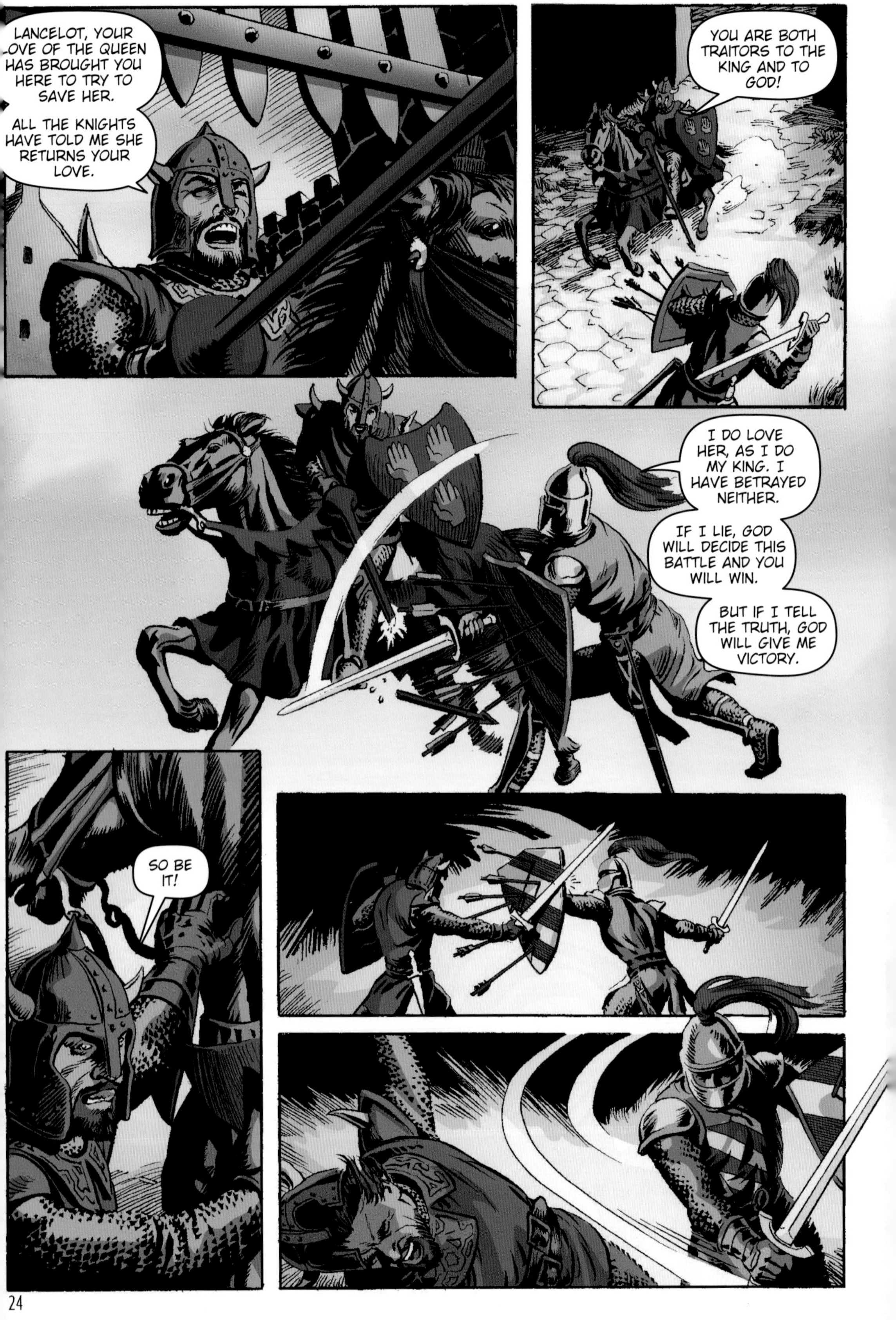
LANCELOT, YOUR LOVE OF THE QUEEN HAS BROUGHT YOU HERE TO TRY TO SAVE HER.
ALL THE KNIGHTS HAVE TOLD ME SHE RETURNS YOUR LOVE.
YOU ARE BOTH TRAITORS TO THE KING AND TO GOD!
I DO LOVE HER, AS I DO MY KING. I HAVE BETRAYED NEITHER.
IF I LIE, GOD WILL DECIDE THIS BATTLE AND YOU WILL WIN.
BUT IF I TELL THE TRUTH, GOD WILL GIVE ME VICTORY.
SO BE IT!

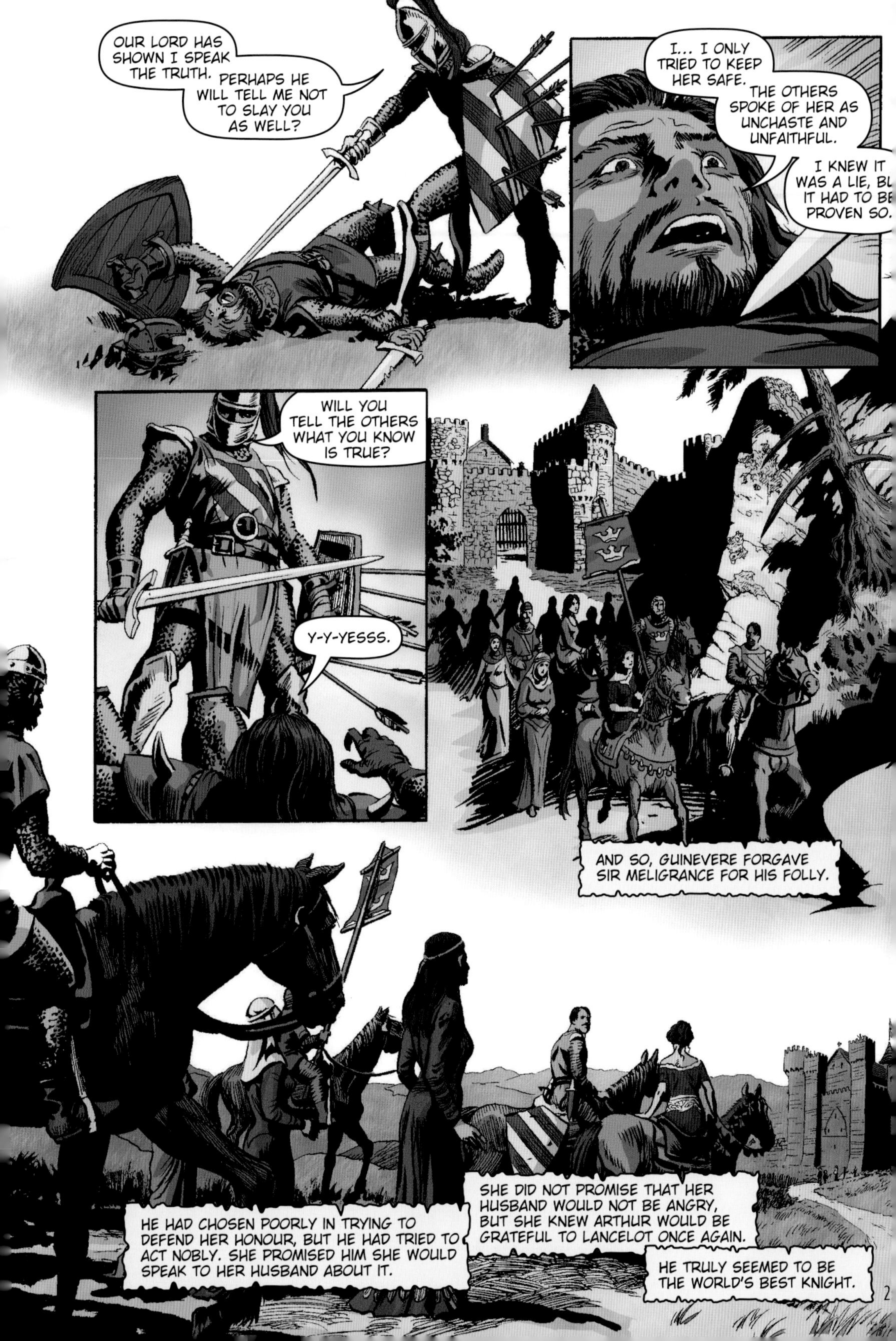
OUR LORD HAS SHOWN I SPEAK THE TRUTH.
PERHAPS HE WILL TELL ME NOT TO SLAY YOU AS WELL?
I... I ONLY TRIED TO KEEP HER SAFE.
THE OTHERS SPOKE OF HER AS UNCHASTE AND UNFAITHFUL.
I KNEW IT WAS A LIE, B IT HAD TO BE PROVEN SO.
WILL YOU TELL THE OTHERS WHAT YOU KNOW IS TRUE?
Y-Y-YESSS.
AND SO, GUINEVERE FORGAVE SIR MELIGRANCE FOR HIS FOLLY.
HE HAD CHOSEN POORLY IN TRYING TO DEFEND HER HONOUR, BUT HE HAD TRIED TO ACT NOBLY. SHE PROMISED HIM SHE WOULD SPEAK TO HER HUSBAND ABOUT IT.
SHE DID NOT PROMISE THAT HER HUSBAND WOULD NOT BE ANGRY, BUT SHE KNEW ARTHUR WOULD BE GRATEFUL TO LANCELOT ONCE AGAIN.
HE TRULY SEEMED TO BE THE WORLD'S BEST KNIGHT.

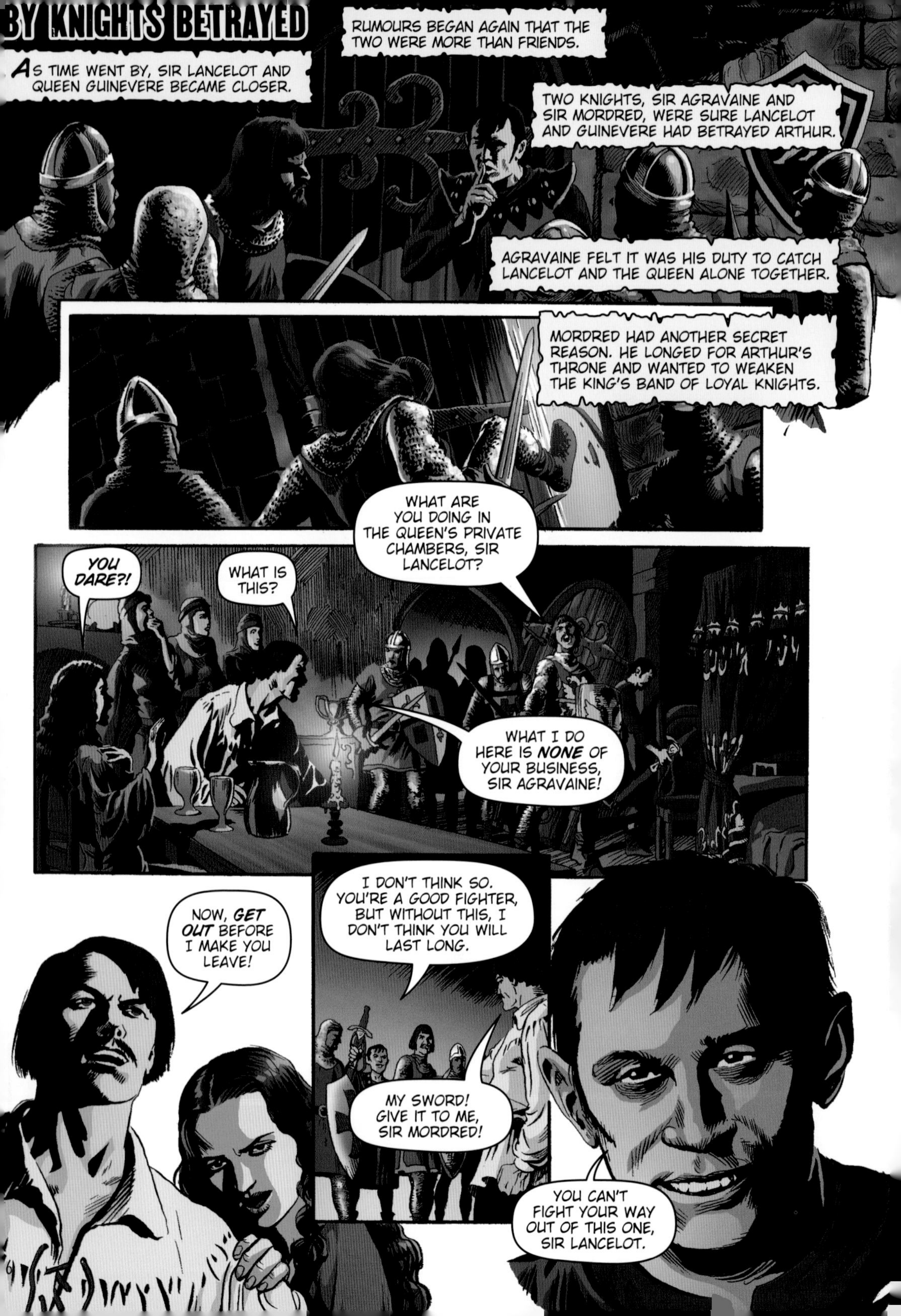
BY KNIGHTS BETRAYED
AS TIME WENT BY, SIR LANCELOT AND QUEEN GUINEVERE BECAME CLOSER.
RUMOURS BEGAN AGAIN THAT THE TWO WERE MORE THAN FRIENDS.
TWO KNIGHTS, SIR AGRAVAINE AND SIR MORDRED, WERE SURE LANCELOT AND GUINEVERE HAD BETRAYED ARTHUR.
AGRAVAINE FELT IT WAS HIS DUTY TO CATCH LANCELOT AND THE QUEEN ALONE TOGETHER.
MORDRED HAD ANOTHER SECRET REASON. HE LONGED FOR ARTHUR'S THRONE AND WANTED TO WEAKEN THE KING'S BAND OF LOYAL KNIGHTS.
WHAT ARE YOU DOING IN THE QUEEN'S PRIVATE CHAMBERS, SIR LANCELOT?
YOU DARE?!
WHAT IS THIS?
WHAT I DO HERE IS NONE OF YOUR BUSINESS, SIR AGRAVAINE!
NOW, GET OUT BEFORE I MAKE YOU LEAVE!
I DON'T THINK SO. YOU'RE A GOOD FIGHTER, BUT WITHOUT THIS, I DON'T THINK YOU WILL LAST LONG.
MY SWORD! GIVE IT TO ME, SIR MORDRED!
YOU CAN'T FIGHT YOUR WAY OUT OF THIS ONE, SIR LANCELOT.

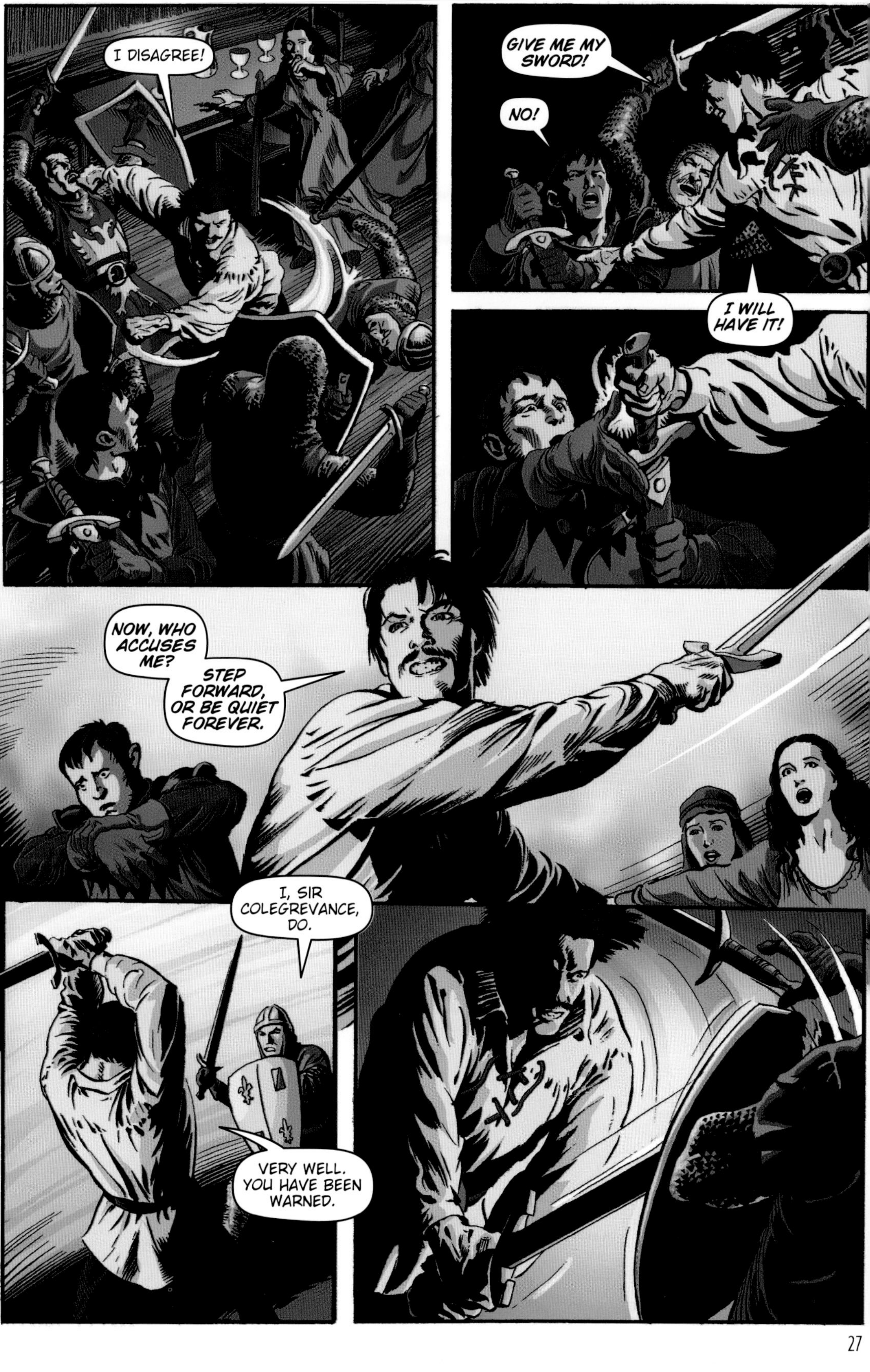
I DISAGREE!
GIVE ME MY SWORD!
NO!
I WILL HAVE IT!
NOW, WHO ACCUSES ME?
STEP FORWARD, OR BE QUIET FOREVER.
I, SIR COLEGREVANCE, DO.
VERY WELL. YOU HAVE BEEN WARNED.

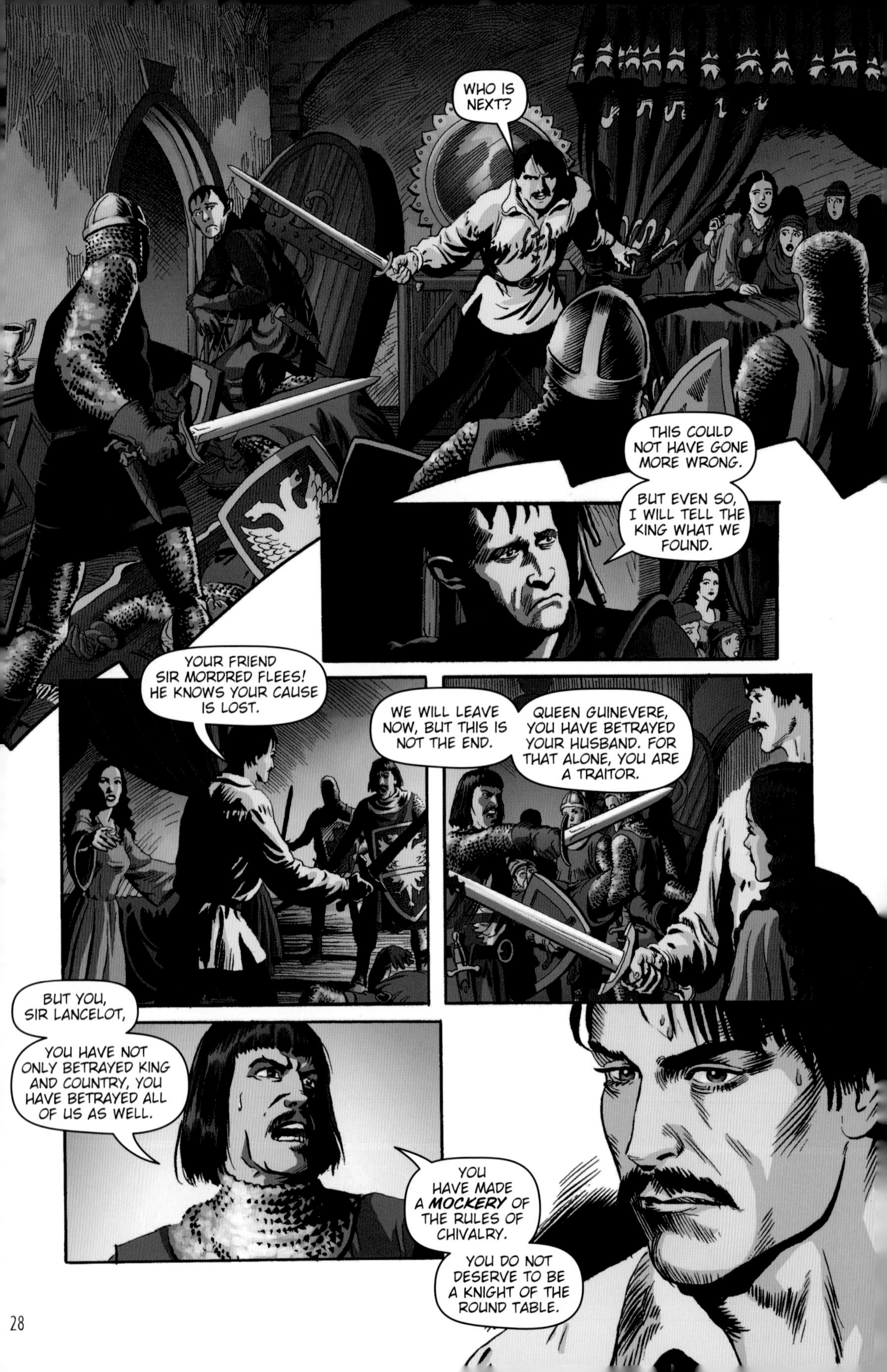
WHO IS NEXT?
THIS COULD NOT HAVE GONE MORE WRONG.
BUT EVEN SO, I WILL TELL THE KING WHAT WE FOUND.
YOUR FRIEND SIR MORDRED FLEES! HE KNOWS YOUR CAUSE IS LOST.
WE WILL LEAVE NOW, BUT THIS IS NOT THE END.
QUEEN GUINEVERE, YOU HAVE BETRAYED YOUR HUSBAND. FOR THAT ALONE, YOU ARE A TRAITOR.
BUT YOU, SIR LANCELOT,
YOU HAVE NOT ONLY BETRAYED KING AND COUNTRY, YOU HAVE BETRAYED ALL OF US AS WELL.
YOU HAVE MADE A ***MOCKERY*** OF THE RULES OF CHIVALRY.
YOU DO NOT DESERVE TO BE A KNIGHT OF THE ROUND TABLE.

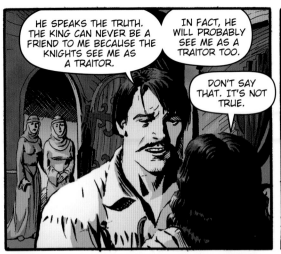

HE SPEAKS THE TRUTH. THE KING CAN NEVER BE A FRIEND TO ME BECAUSE THE KNIGHTS SEE ME AS A TRAITOR.

IN FACT, HE WILL PROBABLY SEE ME AS A TRAITOR TOO.

DON'T SAY THAT. IT'S NOT TRUE.

I'M AFRAID IT IS. I MUST LEAVE CAMELOT.

IF I STAY, THE KING WILL *SLAY* ME.

NO, HE WON'T.

HE MUST. HE IS THE KING, AND HIS RULES MUST BE FOLLOWED.

IF HE ALLOWS ME TO BREAK THE RULES, THEN HE IS NOT A GOOD KING.

BUT IF YOU HAVE BROKEN A RULE, SO HAVE I.

IF HE WOULD SLAY YOU AS A TRAITOR, HE WOULD SLAY ME.

AND IF HE TRIES,

I WILL SAVE YOU.

BUT SIR LANCELOT HOPED HIS LEAVING WOULD ALLOW THE KING TO EXCUSE THE QUEEN. LANCELOT HOPED THAT WITHOUT HIM, CAMELOT WOULD BE HEALED.

29

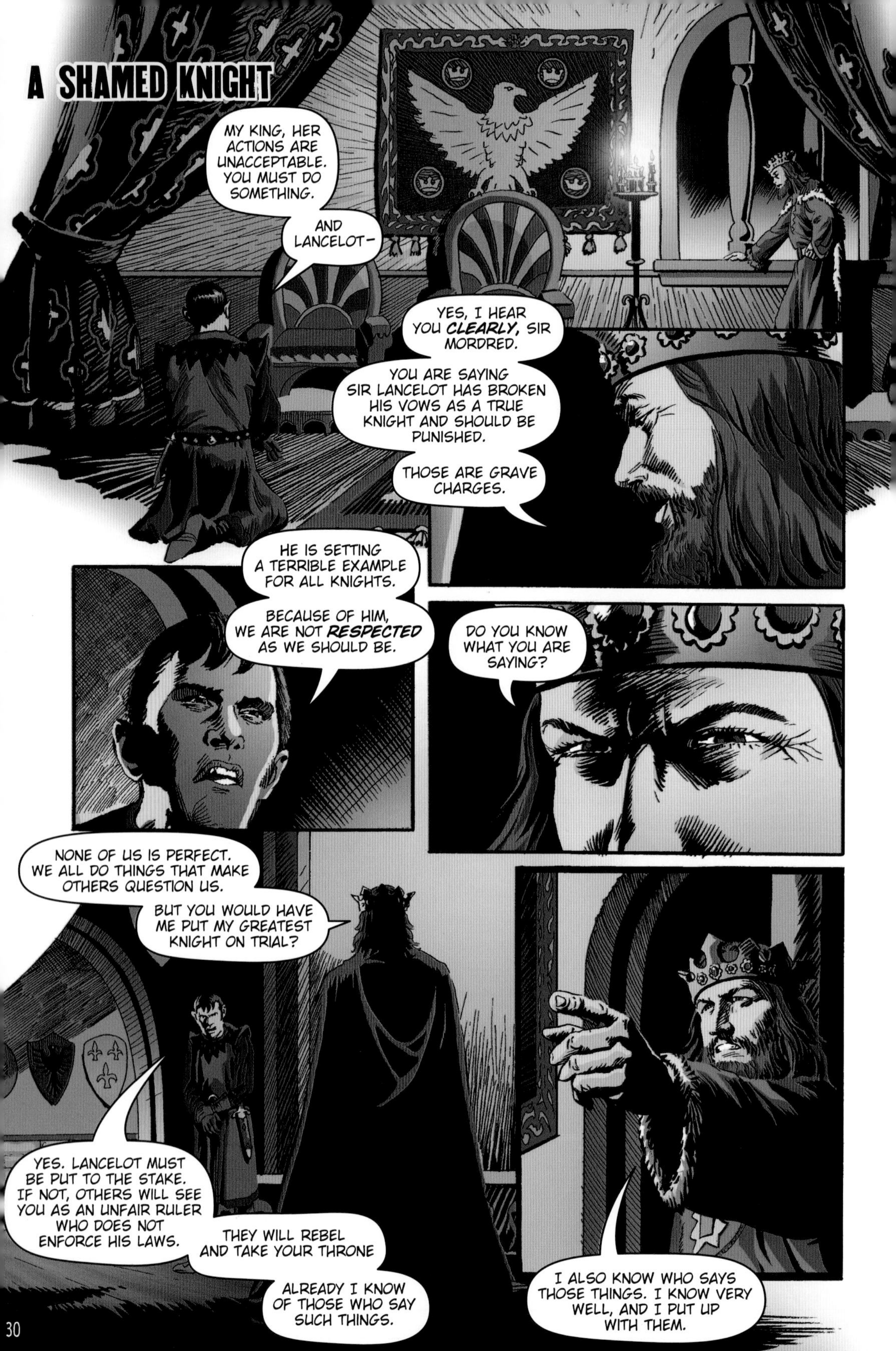
A SHAMED KNIGHT
MY KING, HER ACTIONS ARE UNACCEPTABLE. YOU MUST DO SOMETHING.
AND LANCELOT-
YES, I HEAR YOU CLEARLY, SIR MORDRED.
YOU ARE SAYING SIR LANCELOT HAS BROKEN HIS VOWS AS A TRUE KNIGHT AND SHOULD BE PUNISHED.
THOSE ARE GRAVE CHARGES.
HE IS SETTING A TERRIBLE EXAMPLE FOR ALL KNIGHTS.
BECAUSE OF HIM, WE ARE NOT RESPECTED AS WE SHOULD BE.
DO YOU KNOW WHAT YOU ARE SAYING?
NONE OF US IS PERFECT. WE ALL DO THINGS THAT MAKE OTHERS QUESTION US.
BUT YOU WOULD HAVE ME PUT MY GREATEST KNIGHT ON TRIAL?
YES. LANCELOT MUST BE PUT TO THE STAKE. IF NOT, OTHERS WILL SEE YOU AS AN UNFAIR RULER WHO DOES NOT ENFORCE HIS LAWS.
THEY WILL REBEL AND TAKE YOUR THRONE
ALREADY I KNOW OF THOSE WHO SAY SUCH THINGS.
I ALSO KNOW WHO SAYS THOSE THINGS. I KNOW VERY WELL, AND I PUT UP WITH THEM.

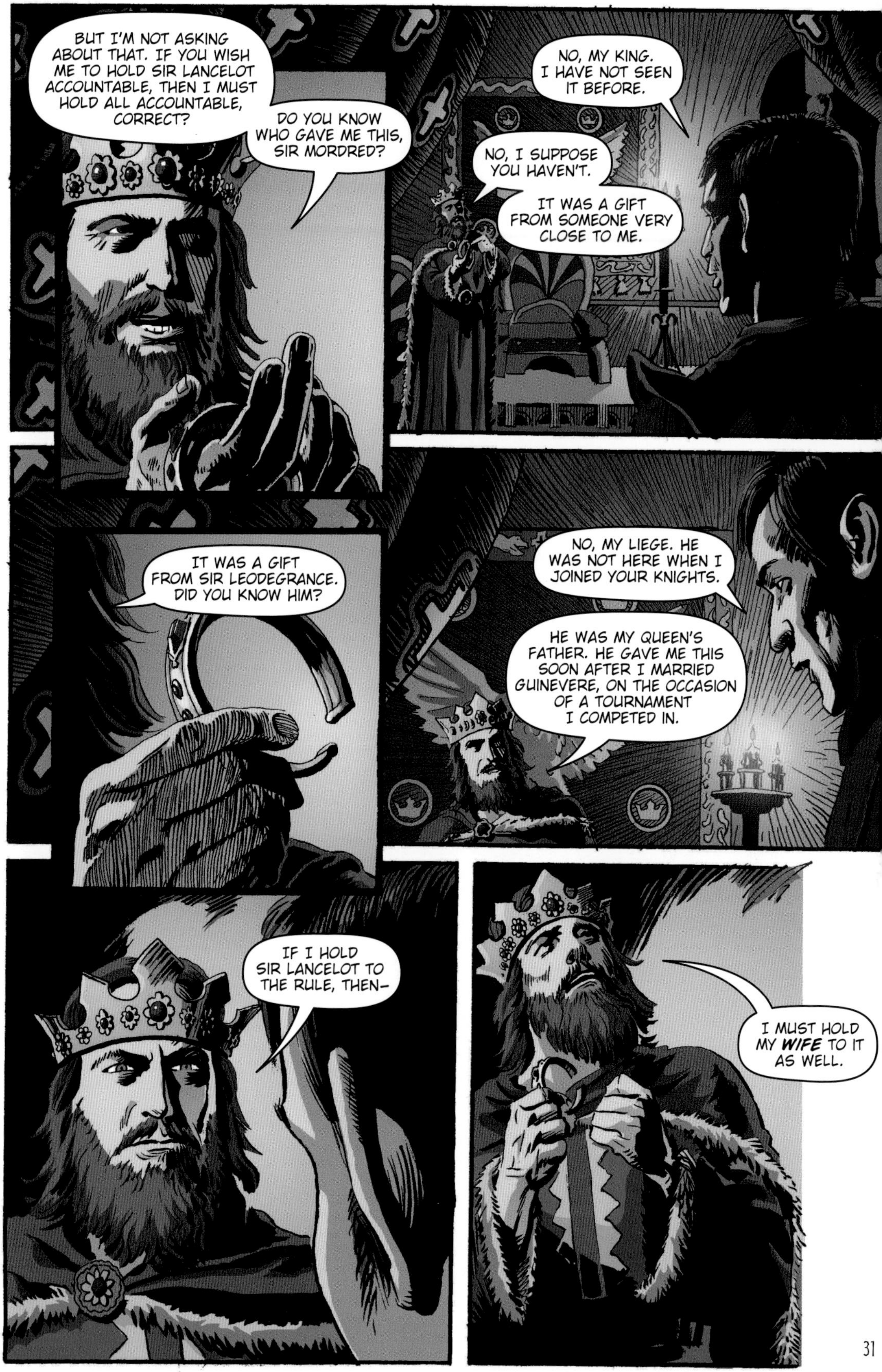
BUT I'M NOT ASKING ABOUT THAT. IF YOU WISH ME TO HOLD SIR LANCELOT ACCOUNTABLE, THEN I MUST HOLD ALL ACCOUNTABLE, CORRECT?
DO YOU KNOW WHO GAVE ME THIS, SIR MORDRED?
NO, MY KING. I HAVE NOT SEEN IT BEFORE.
NO, I SUPPOSE YOU HAVEN'T.
IT WAS A GIFT FROM SOMEONE VERY CLOSE TO ME.
IT WAS A GIFT FROM SIR LEODEGRANCE. DID YOU KNOW HIM?
NO, MY LIEGE. HE WAS NOT HERE WHEN I JOINED YOUR KNIGHTS.
HE WAS MY QUEEN'S FATHER. HE GAVE ME THIS SOON AFTER I MARRIED GUINEVERE, ON THE OCCASION OF A TOURNAMENT I COMPETED IN.
IF I HOLD SIR LANCELOT TO THE RULE, THEN–
I MUST HOLD MY ***WIFE*** TO IT AS WELL.

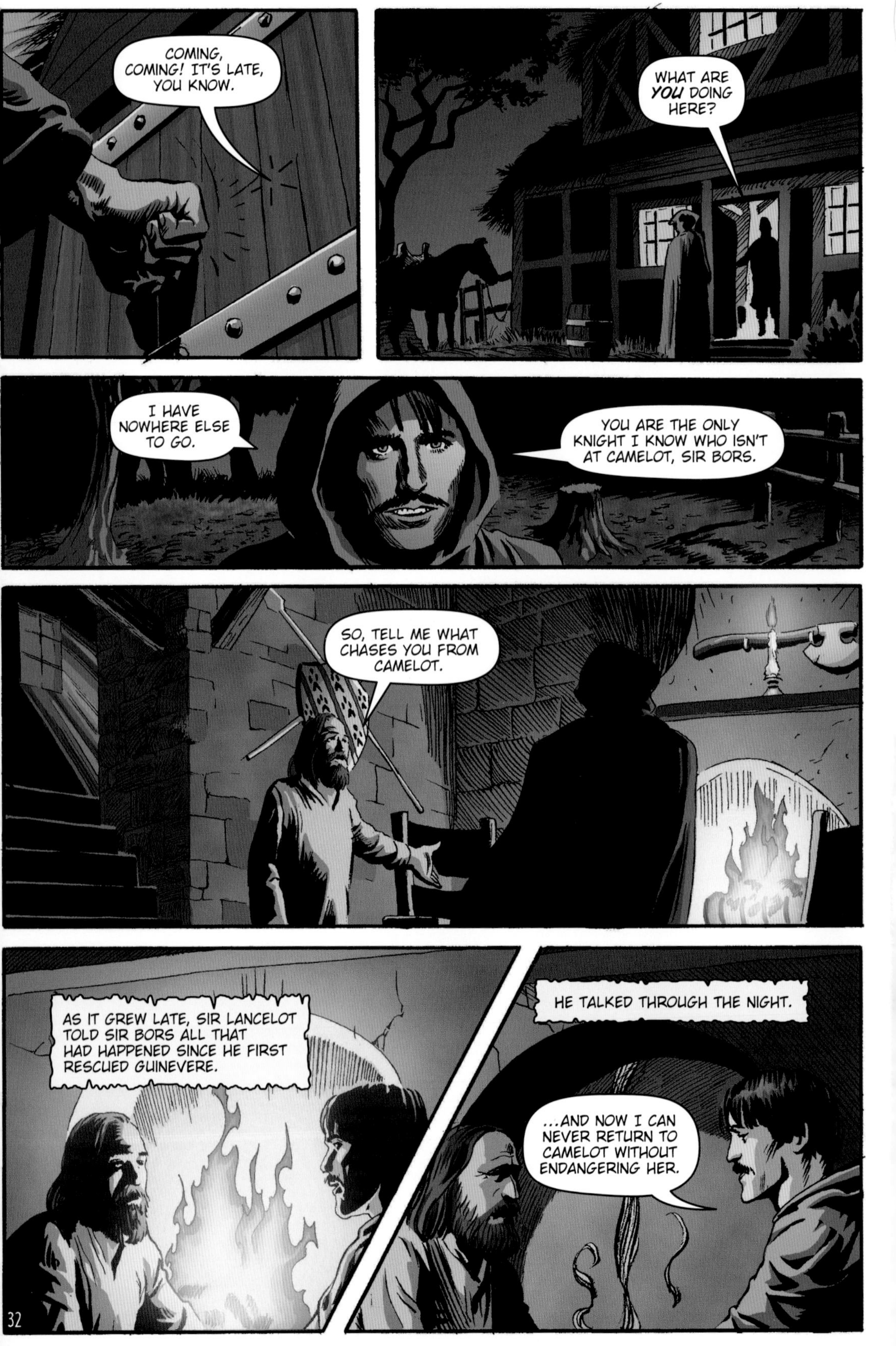

COMING, COMING! IT'S LATE, YOU KNOW.
WHAT ARE ***YOU*** DOING HERE?
I HAVE NOWHERE ELSE TO GO.
YOU ARE THE ONLY KNIGHT I KNOW WHO ISN'T AT CAMELOT, SIR BORS.
SO, TELL ME WHAT CHASES YOU FROM CAMELOT.
AS IT GREW LATE, SIR LANCELOT TOLD SIR BORS ALL THAT HAD HAPPENED SINCE HE FIRST RESCUED GUINEVERE.
HE TALKED THROUGH THE NIGHT.
...AND NOW I CAN NEVER RETURN TO CAMELOT WITHOUT ENDANGERING HER.

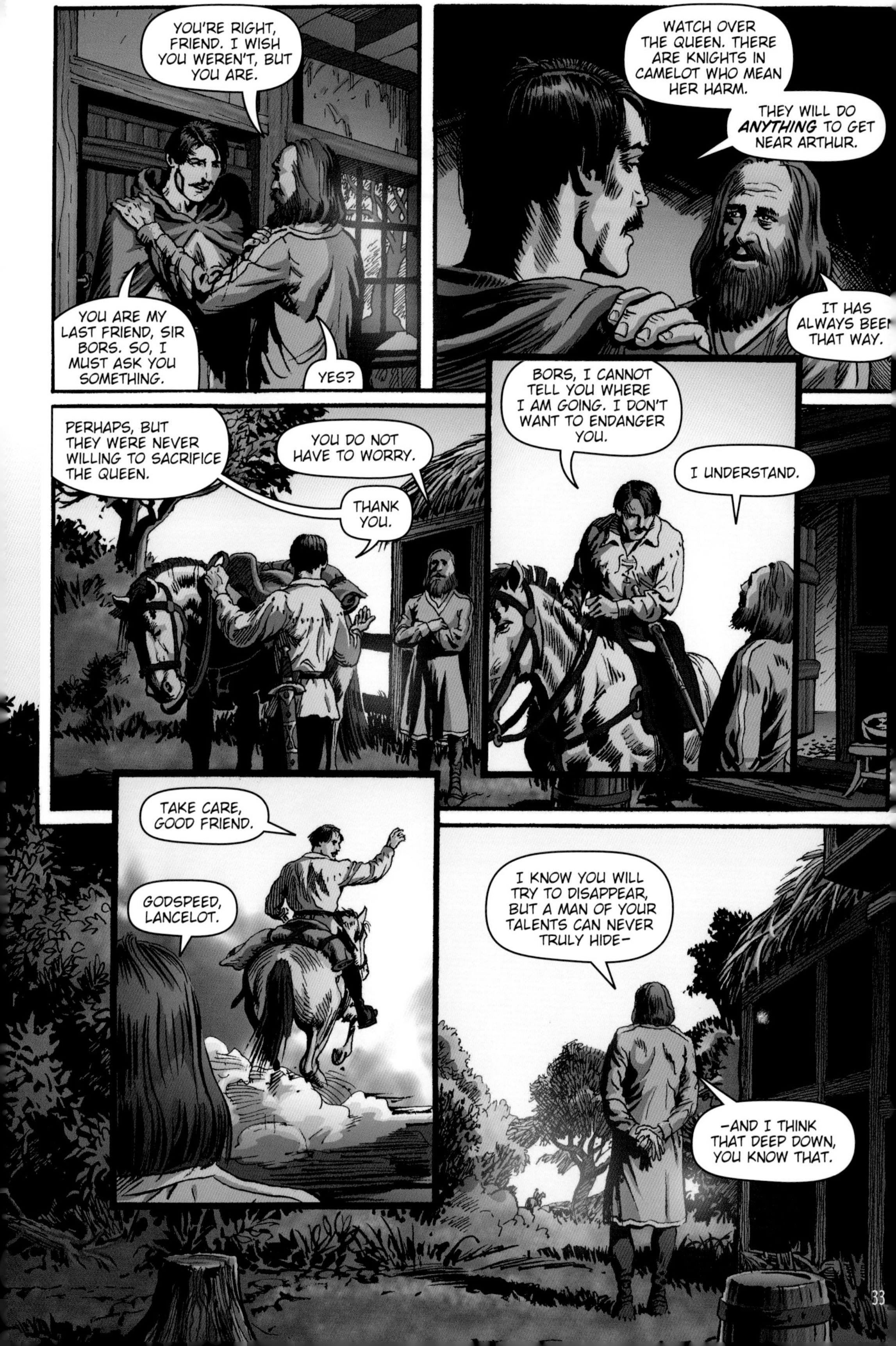
YOU'RE RIGHT, FRIEND. I WISH YOU WEREN'T, BUT YOU ARE.
YOU ARE MY LAST FRIEND, SIR BORS. SO, I MUST ASK YOU SOMETHING.
YES?
WATCH OVER THE QUEEN. THERE ARE KNIGHTS IN CAMELOT WHO MEAN HER HARM.
THEY WILL DO ANYTHING TO GET NEAR ARTHUR.
IT HAS ALWAYS BEEN THAT WAY.
PERHAPS, BUT THEY WERE NEVER WILLING TO SACRIFICE THE QUEEN.
YOU DO NOT HAVE TO WORRY.
THANK YOU.
BORS, I CANNOT TELL YOU WHERE I AM GOING. I DON'T WANT TO ENDANGER YOU.
I UNDERSTAND.
TAKE CARE, GOOD FRIEND.
GODSPEED, LANCELOT.
I KNOW YOU WILL TRY TO DISAPPEAR, BUT A MAN OF YOUR TALENTS CAN NEVER TRULY HIDE–
–AND I THINK THAT DEEP DOWN, YOU KNOW THAT.

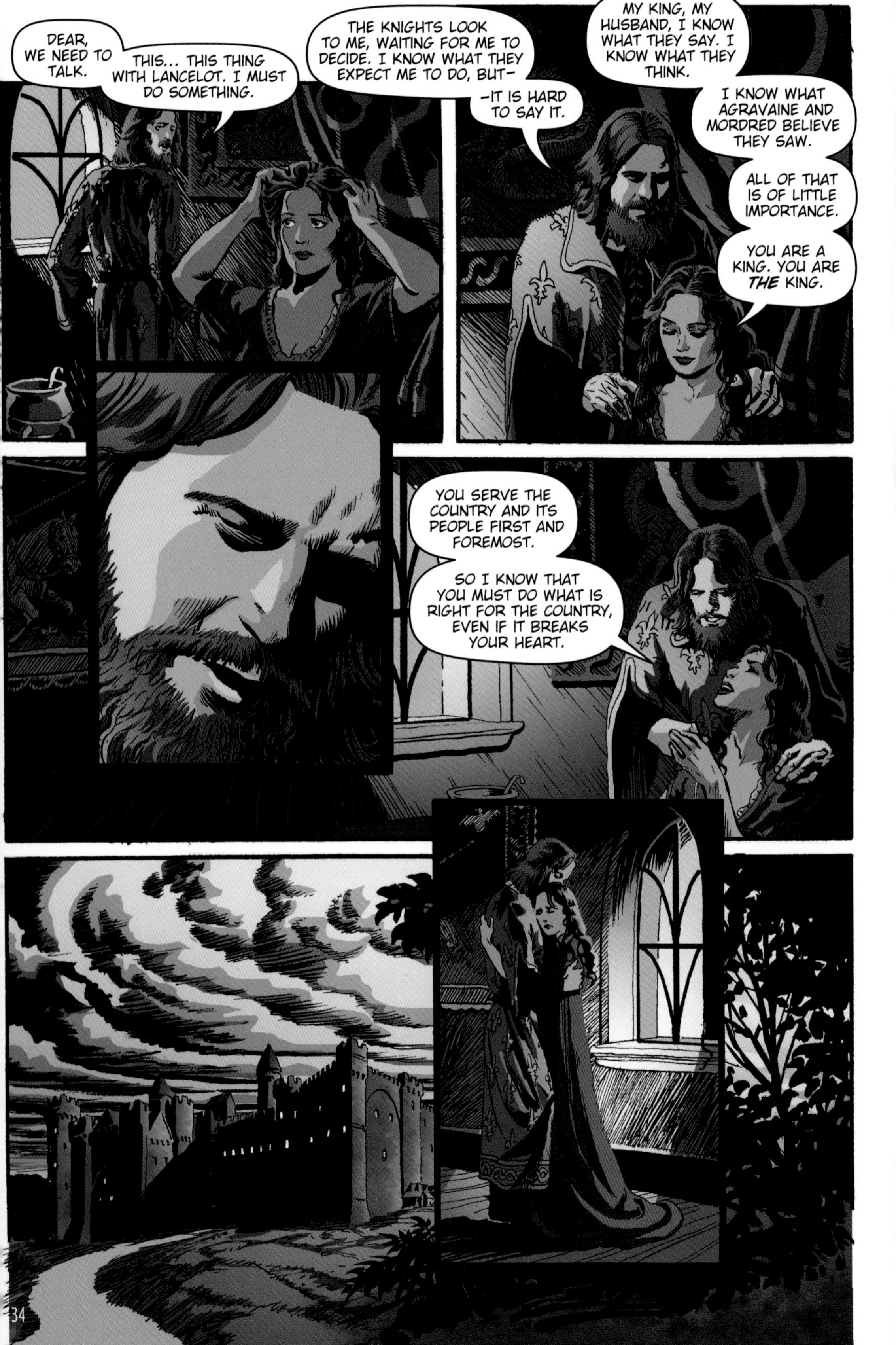
DEAR, WE NEED TO TALK.
THIS... THIS THING WITH LANCELOT. I MUST DO SOMETHING.
THE KNIGHTS LOOK TO ME, WAITING FOR ME TO DECIDE. I KNOW WHAT THEY EXPECT ME TO DO, BUT-
-IT IS HARD TO SAY IT.
MY KING, MY HUSBAND, I KNOW WHAT THEY SAY. I KNOW WHAT THEY THINK.
I KNOW WHAT AGRAVAINE AND MORDRED BELIEVE THEY SAW.
ALL OF THAT IS OF LITTLE IMPORTANCE.
YOU ARE A KING. YOU ARE *THE* KING.
YOU SERVE THE COUNTRY AND ITS PEOPLE FIRST AND FOREMOST.
SO I KNOW THAT YOU MUST DO WHAT IS RIGHT FOR THE COUNTRY, EVEN IF IT BREAKS YOUR HEART.

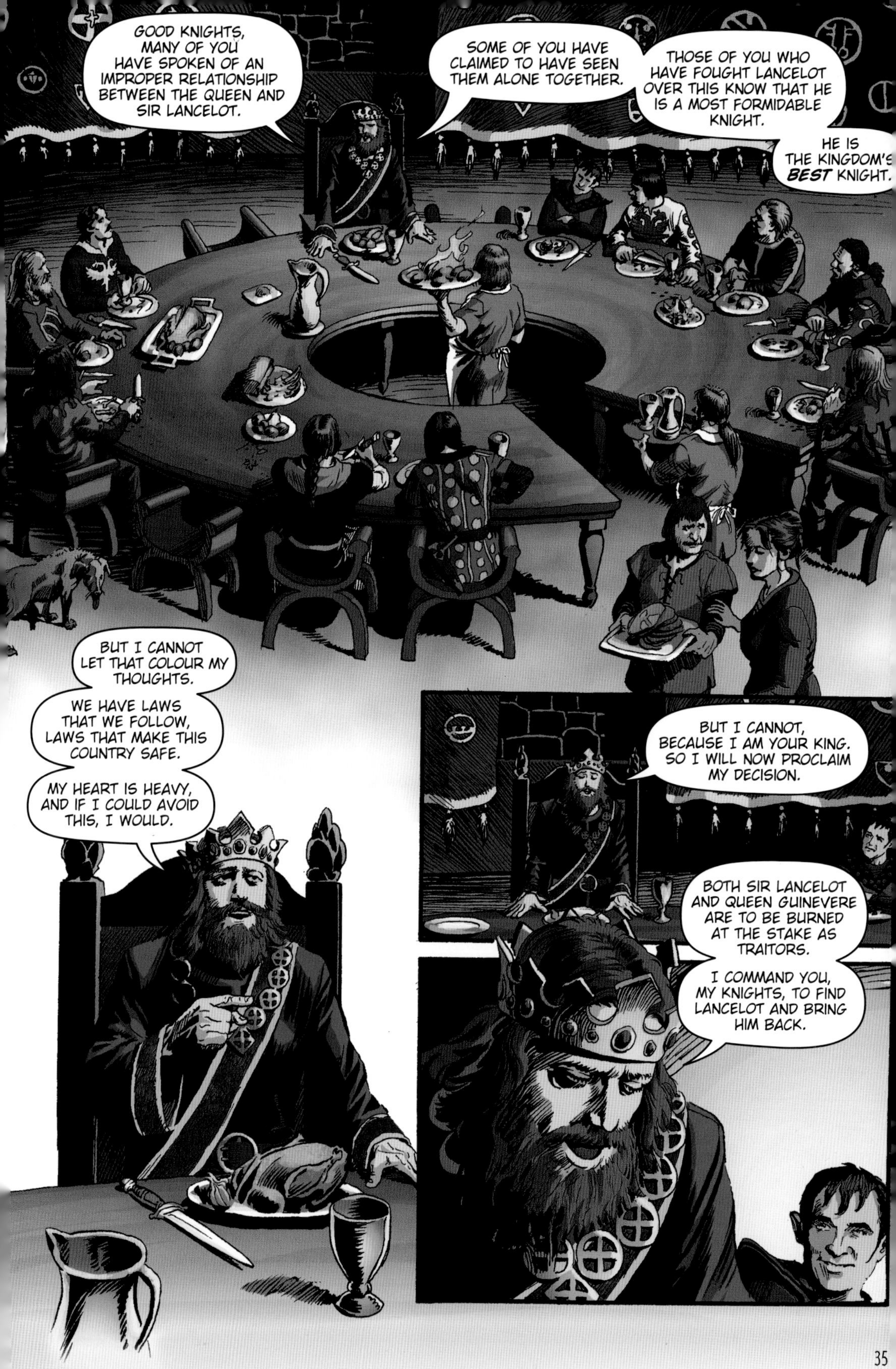
GOOD KNIGHTS, MANY OF YOU HAVE SPOKEN OF AN IMPROPER RELATIONSHIP BETWEEN THE QUEEN AND SIR LANCELOT.
SOME OF YOU HAVE CLAIMED TO HAVE SEEN THEM ALONE TOGETHER.
THOSE OF YOU WHO HAVE FOUGHT LANCELOT OVER THIS KNOW THAT HE IS A MOST FORMIDABLE KNIGHT.
HE IS THE KINGDOM'S BEST KNIGHT.
BUT I CANNOT LET THAT COLOUR MY THOUGHTS.
WE HAVE LAWS THAT WE FOLLOW, LAWS THAT MAKE THIS COUNTRY SAFE.
MY HEART IS HEAVY, AND IF I COULD AVOID THIS, I WOULD.
BUT I CANNOT, BECAUSE I AM YOUR KING. SO I WILL NOW PROCLAIM MY DECISION.
BOTH SIR LANCELOT AND QUEEN GUINEVERE ARE TO BE BURNED AT THE STAKE AS TRAITORS.
I COMMAND YOU, MY KNIGHTS, TO FIND LANCELOT AND BRING HIM BACK.

THE-SEARCH-FOR-SIR-LANCELOT

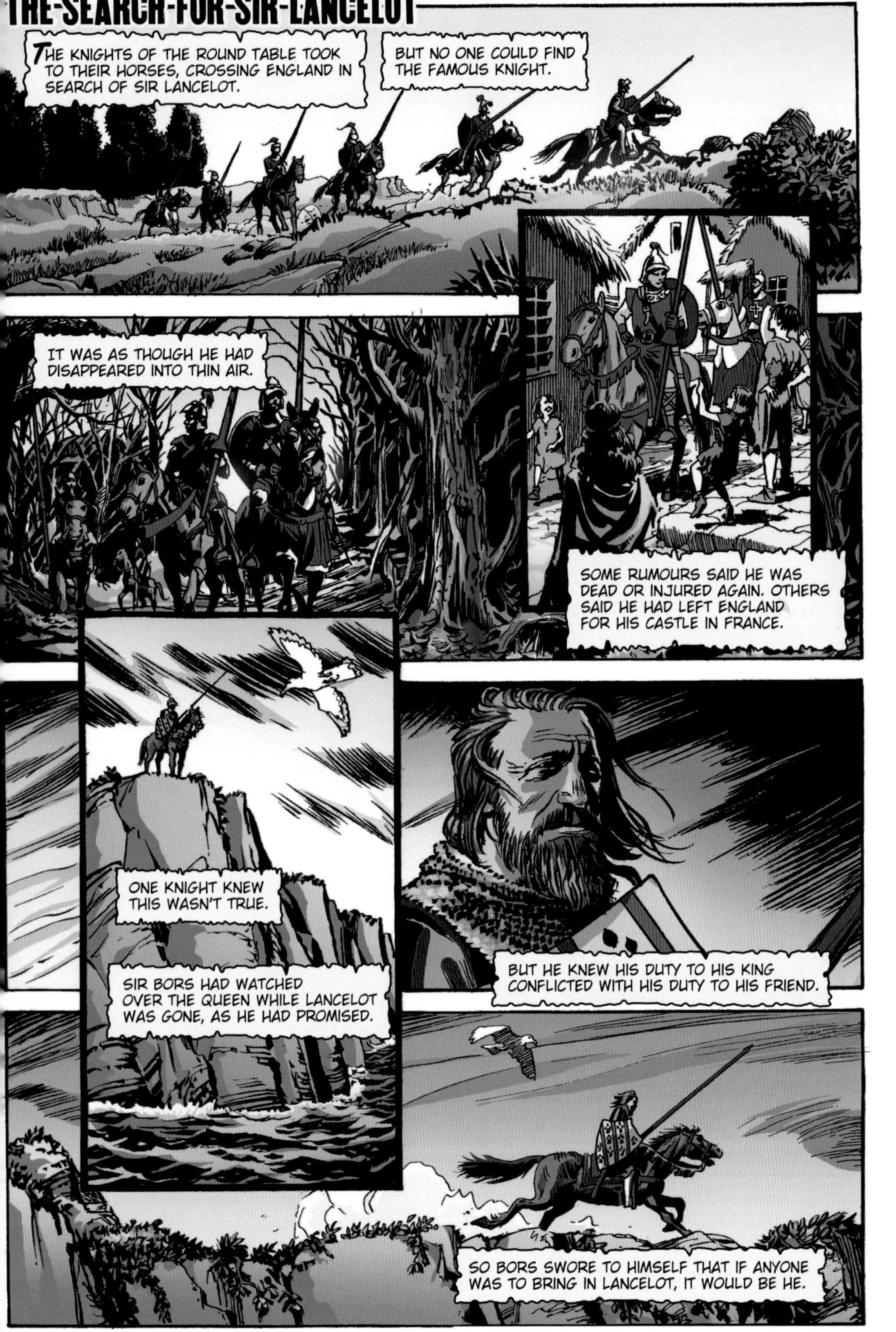
THE KNIGHTS OF THE ROUND TABLE TOOK TO THEIR HORSES, CROSSING ENGLAND IN SEARCH OF SIR LANCELOT.
BUT NO ONE COULD FIND THE FAMOUS KNIGHT.
IT WAS AS THOUGH HE HAD DISAPPEARED INTO THIN AIR.
SOME RUMOURS SAID HE WAS DEAD OR INJURED AGAIN. OTHERS SAID HE HAD LEFT ENGLAND FOR HIS CASTLE IN FRANCE.
ONE KNIGHT KNEW THIS WASN'T TRUE.
SIR BORS HAD WATCHED OVER THE QUEEN WHILE LANCELOT WAS GONE, AS HE HAD PROMISED.
BUT HE KNEW HIS DUTY TO HIS KING CONFLICTED WITH HIS DUTY TO HIS FRIEND.
SO BORS SWORE TO HIMSELF THAT IF ANYONE WAS TO BRING IN LANCELOT, IT WOULD BE HE.

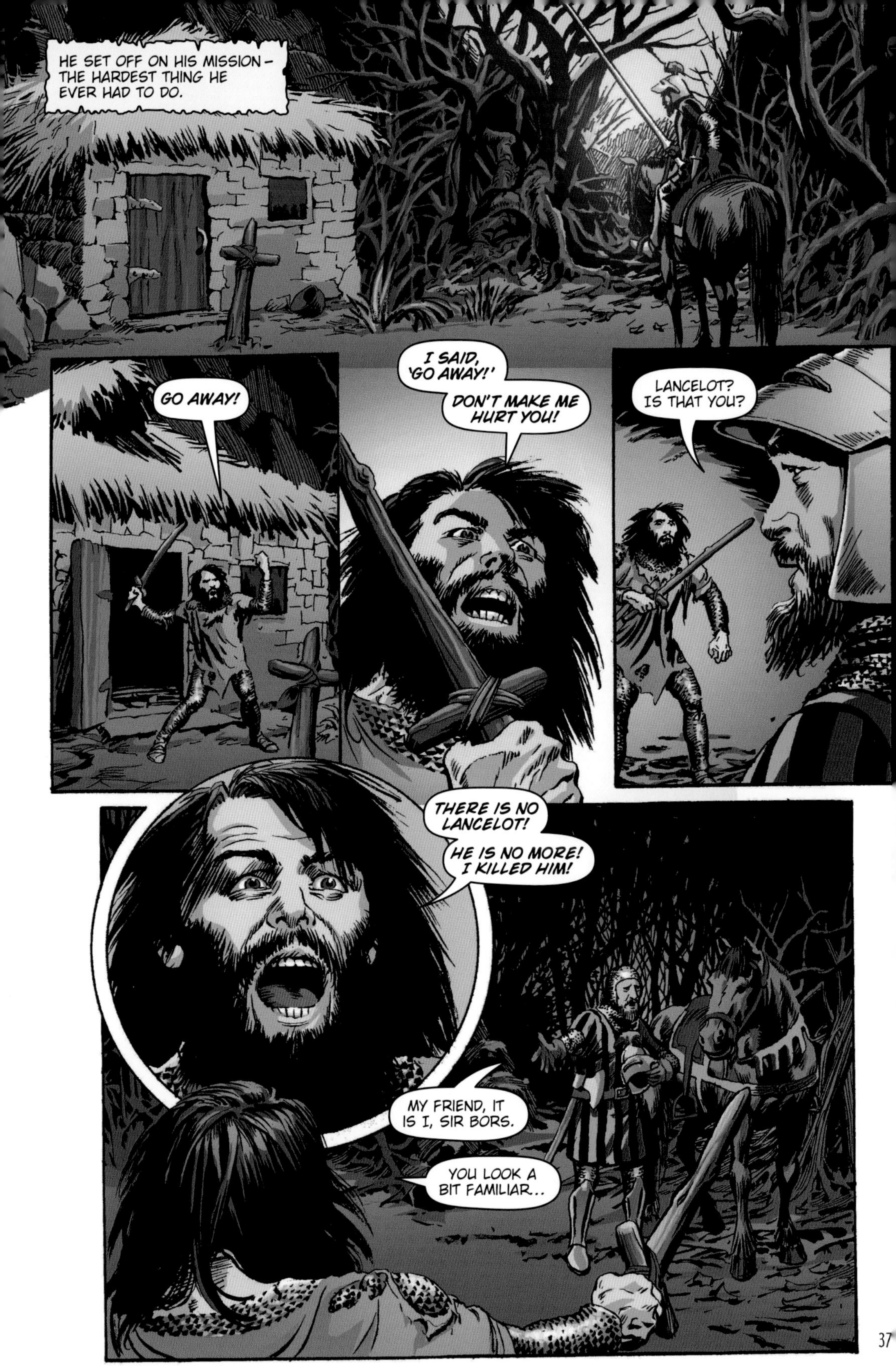
HE SET OFF ON HIS MISSION – THE HARDEST THING HE EVER HAD TO DO.
GO AWAY!
I SAID, 'GO AWAY!'
DON'T MAKE ME HURT YOU!
LANCELOT? IS THAT YOU?
THERE IS NO LANCELOT!
HE IS NO MORE! I KILLED HIM!
MY FRIEND, IT IS I, SIR BORS.
YOU LOOK A BIT FAMILIAR..

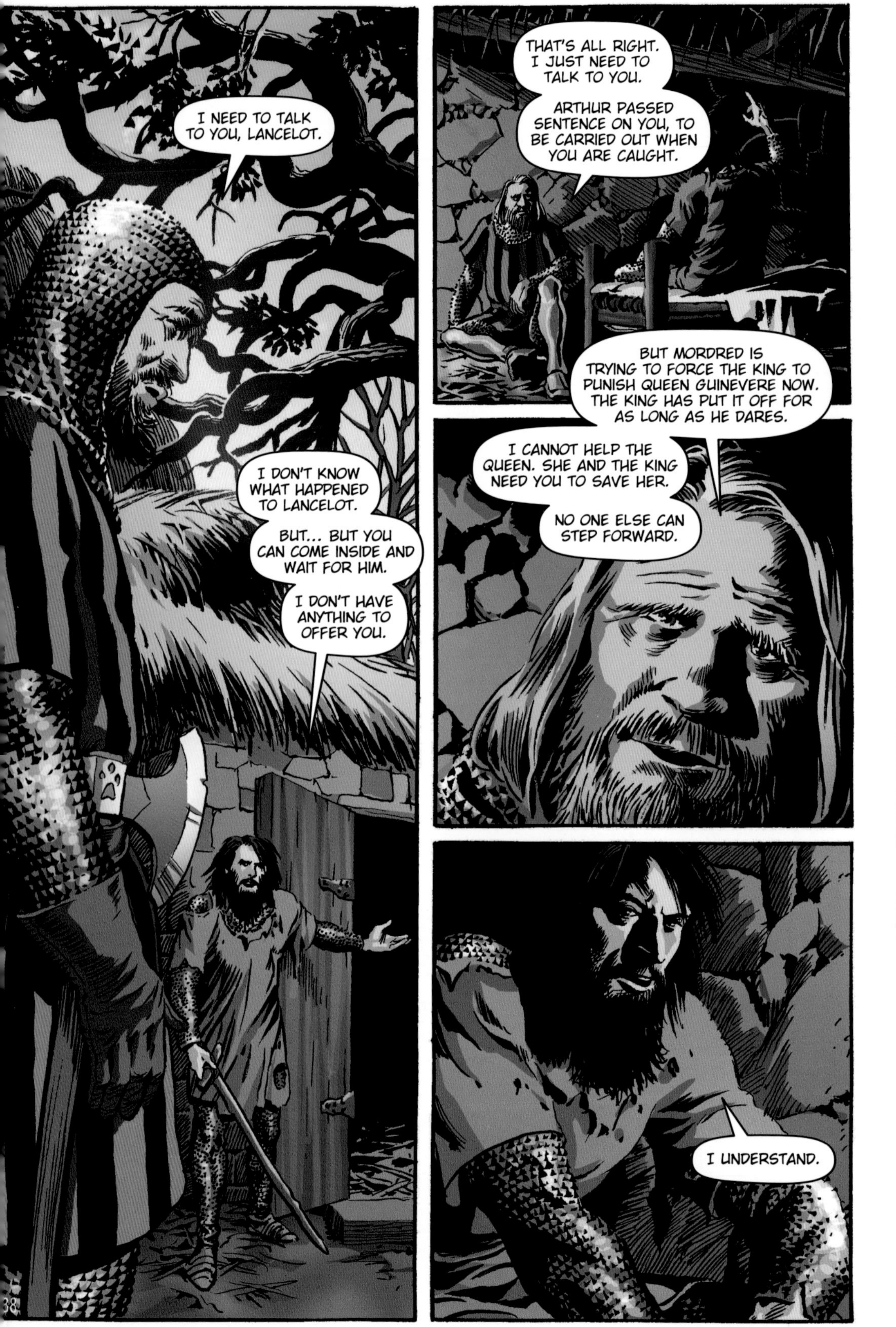
I NEED TO TALK TO YOU, LANCELOT.
I DON'T KNOW WHAT HAPPENED TO LANCELOT.
BUT... BUT YOU CAN COME INSIDE AND WAIT FOR HIM.
I DON'T HAVE ANYTHING TO OFFER YOU.
THAT'S ALL RIGHT. I JUST NEED TO TALK TO YOU.
ARTHUR PASSED SENTENCE ON YOU, TO BE CARRIED OUT WHEN YOU ARE CAUGHT.
BUT MORDRED IS TRYING TO FORCE THE KING TO PUNISH QUEEN GUINEVERE NOW. THE KING HAS PUT IT OFF FOR AS LONG AS HE DARES.
I CANNOT HELP THE QUEEN. SHE AND THE KING NEED YOU TO SAVE HER.
NO ONE ELSE CAN STEP FORWARD.
I UNDERSTAND.

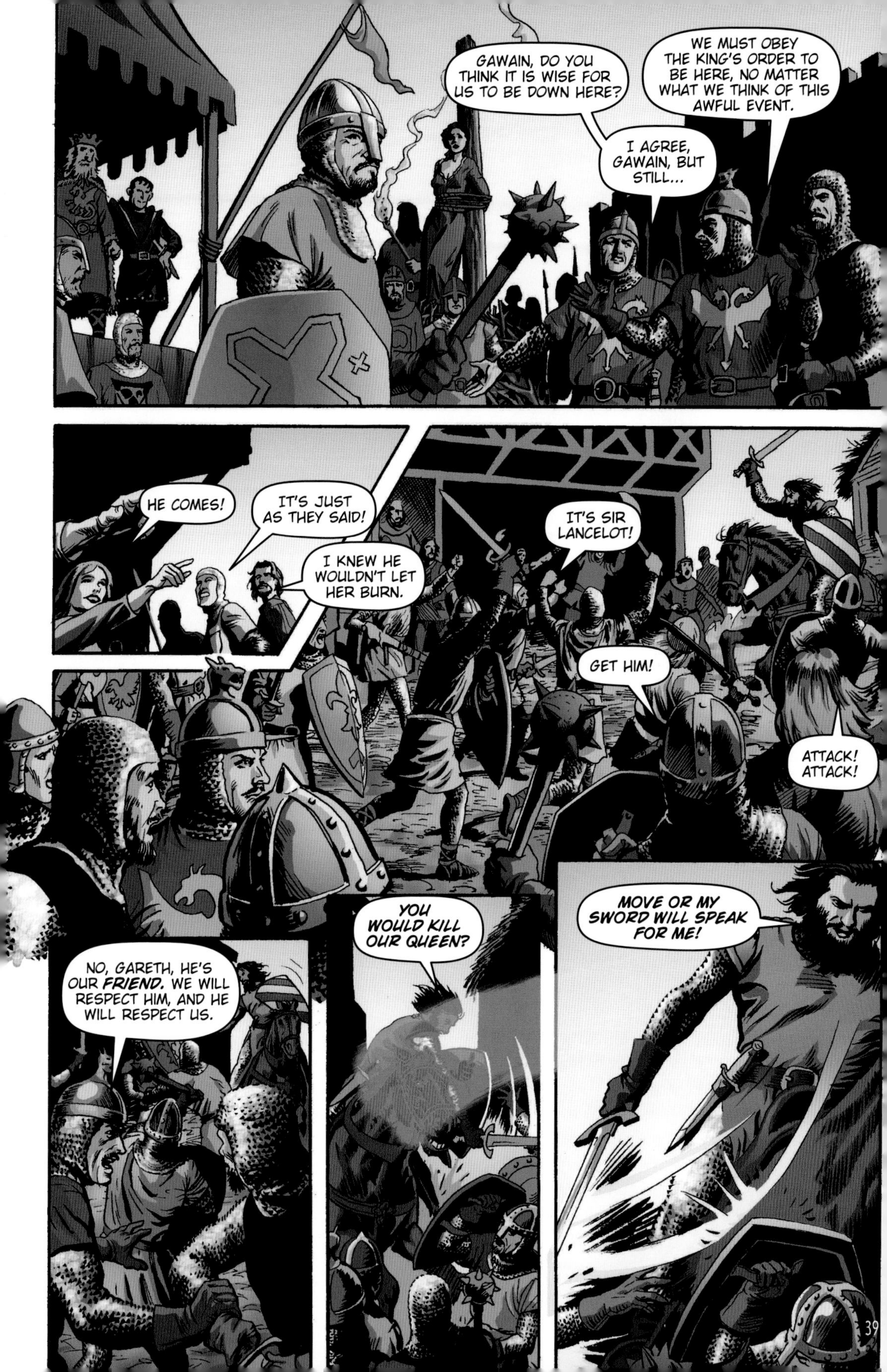
GAWAIN, DO YOU THINK IT IS WISE FOR US TO BE DOWN HERE?
WE MUST OBEY THE KING'S ORDER TO BE HERE, NO MATTER WHAT WE THINK OF THIS AWFUL EVENT.
I AGREE, GAWAIN, BUT STILL...
HE COMES!
IT'S JUST AS THEY SAID!
I KNEW HE WOULDN'T LET HER BURN.
IT'S SIR LANCELOT!
GET HIM!
ATTACK! ATTACK!
NO, GARETH, HE'S OUR FRIEND. WE WILL RESPECT HIM, AND HE WILL RESPECT US.
YOU WOULD KILL OUR QUEEN?
MOVE OR MY SWORD WILL SPEAK FOR ME!

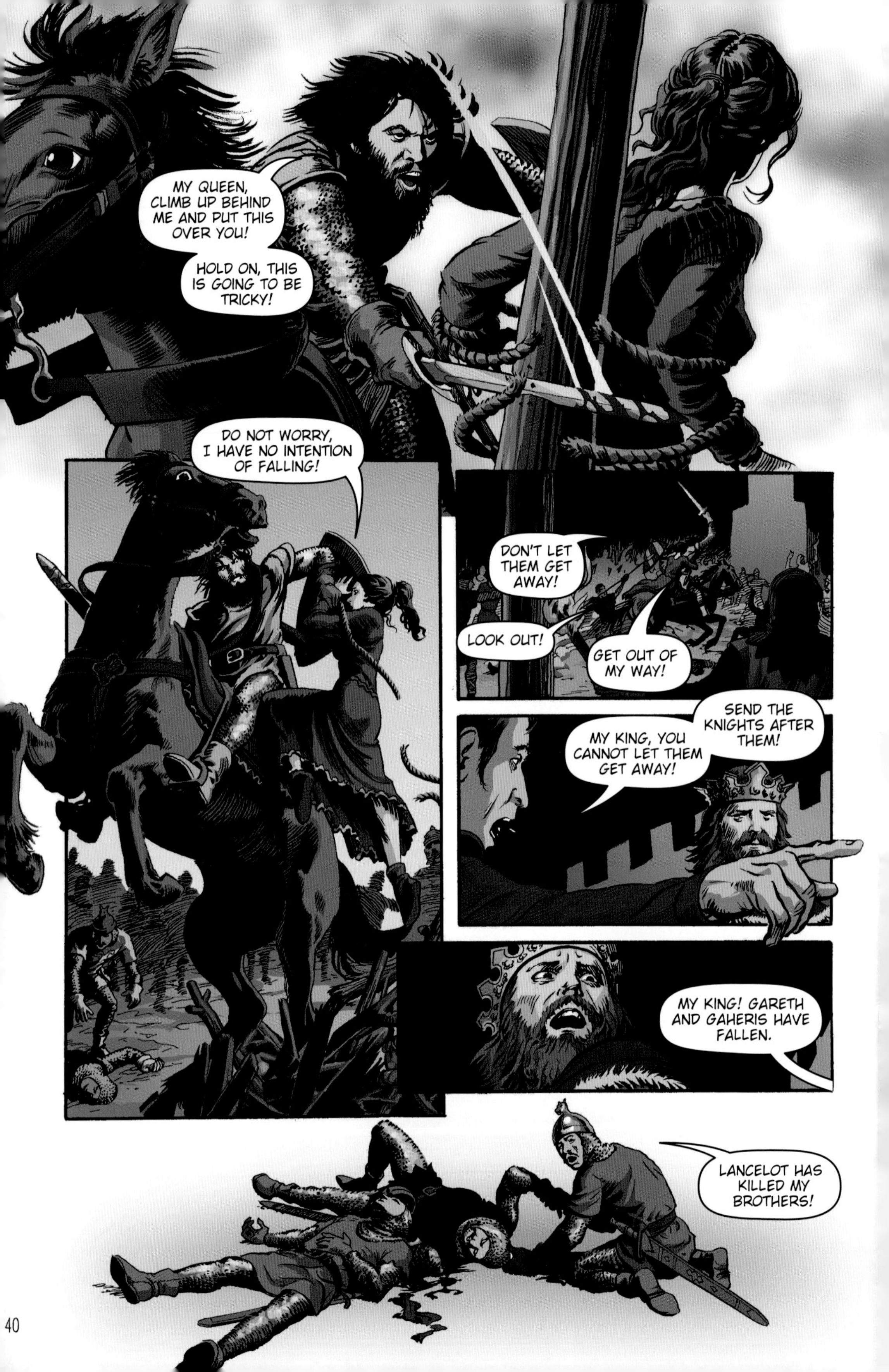
MY QUEEN, CLIMB UP BEHIND ME AND PUT THIS OVER YOU!
HOLD ON, THIS IS GOING TO BE TRICKY!
DO NOT WORRY, I HAVE NO INTENTION OF FALLING!
DON'T LET THEM GET AWAY!
LOOK OUT!
GET OUT OF MY WAY!
MY KING, YOU CANNOT LET THEM GET AWAY!
SEND THE KNIGHTS AFTER THEM!
MY KING! GARETH AND GAHERIS HAVE FALLEN.
LANCELOT HAS KILLED MY BROTHERS!

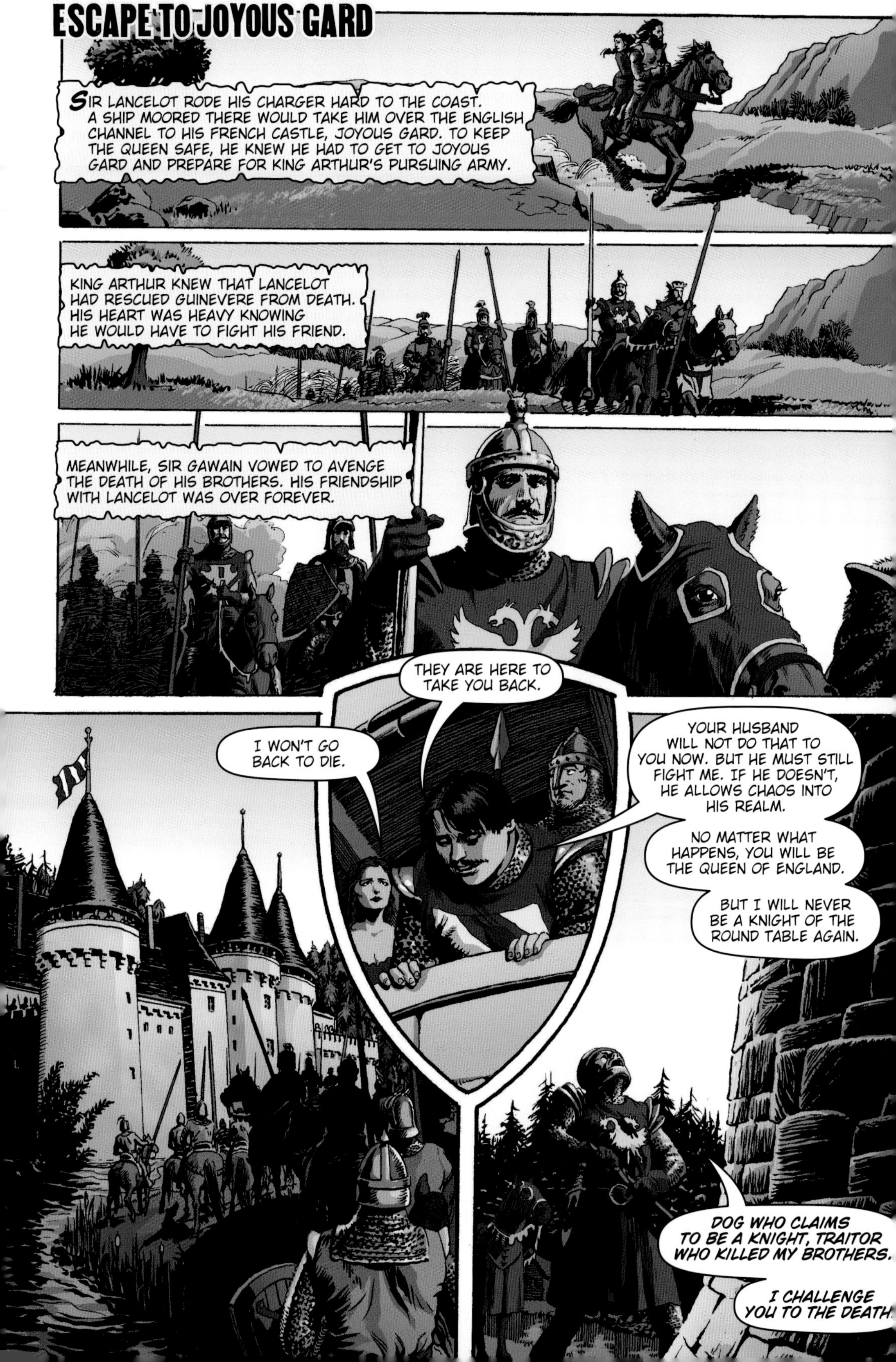
ESCAPE TO JOYOUS GARD
SIR LANCELOT RODE HIS CHARGER HARD TO THE COAST. A SHIP MOORED THERE WOULD TAKE HIM OVER THE ENGLISH CHANNEL TO HIS FRENCH CASTLE, JOYOUS GARD. TO KEEP THE QUEEN SAFE, HE KNEW HE HAD TO GET TO JOYOUS GARD AND PREPARE FOR KING ARTHUR'S PURSUING ARMY.
KING ARTHUR KNEW THAT LANCELOT HAD RESCUED GUINEVERE FROM DEATH. HIS HEART WAS HEAVY KNOWING HE WOULD HAVE TO FIGHT HIS FRIEND.
MEANWHILE, SIR GAWAIN VOWED TO AVENGE THE DEATH OF HIS BROTHERS. HIS FRIENDSHIP WITH LANCELOT WAS OVER FOREVER.
THEY ARE HERE TO TAKE YOU BACK.
I WON'T GO BACK TO DIE.
YOUR HUSBAND WILL NOT DO THAT TO YOU NOW. BUT HE MUST STILL FIGHT ME. IF HE DOESN'T, HE ALLOWS CHAOS INTO HIS REALM.
NO MATTER WHAT HAPPENS, YOU WILL BE THE QUEEN OF ENGLAND.
BUT I WILL NEVER BE A KNIGHT OF THE ROUND TABLE AGAIN.
DOG WHO CLAIMS TO BE A KNIGHT, TRAITOR WHO KILLED MY BROTHERS.
I CHALLENGE YOU TO THE DEATH.

COME DOWN, LANCELOT. MEET ME IN THE MIDDLE OF THIS FIELD AND END THIS WAR.

GOD DEFEND ME THAT I SHOULD FIGHT MY MOST NOBLE KING.

NO, I AM YOUR ENEMY NOW.

YOU HAVE KILLED MANY OF MY GOOD KNIGHTS.

YOU HAVE KIDNAPPED MY QUEEN.

WE ARE NO LONGER FRIENDS.

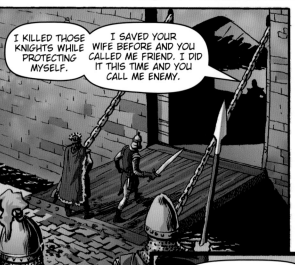

I KILLED THOSE KNIGHTS WHILE PROTECTING MYSELF.

I SAVED YOUR WIFE BEFORE AND YOU CALLED ME FRIEND. I DID IT THIS TIME AND YOU CALL ME ENEMY.

SHE IS MY WIFE, AND YOU WERE IN HER CHAMBERS.

I WILL FIGHT ANYONE WHO SAYS I DID SOMETHING IMPROPER WITH HER.

I TOOK HER AWAY ONLY BECAUSE YOU WERE GOING TO HAVE HER KILLED.

LIAR! YOU KILLED MY BROTHERS AND KIDNAPPED THE QUEEN BECAUSE YOU WANTED HER.

I WILL HAVE YOUR HEAD!

NO.

LANCELOT AND I WILL SETTLE THIS BETWEEN US.

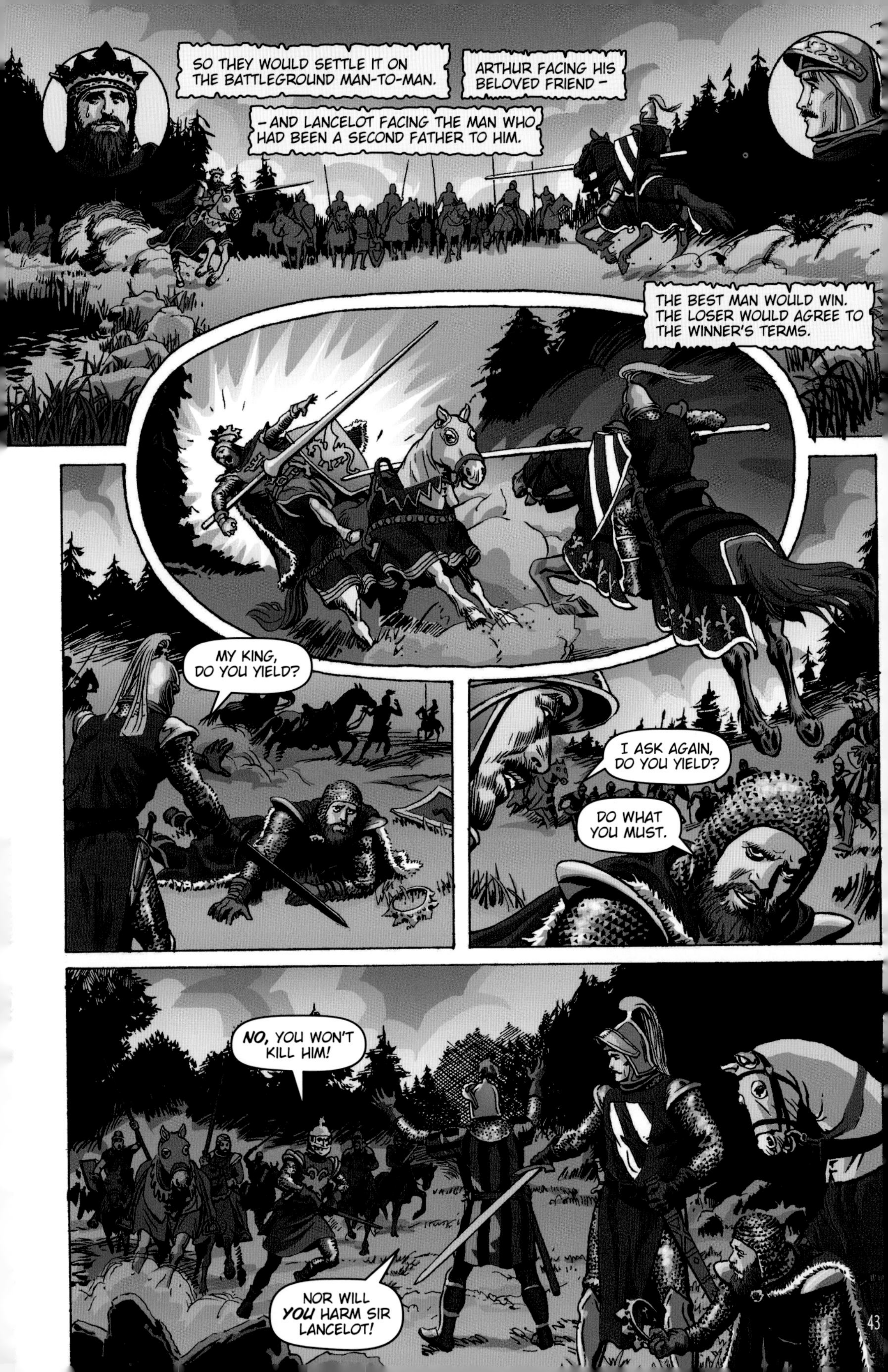
SO THEY WOULD SETTLE IT ON THE BATTLEGROUND MAN-TO-MAN.
ARTHUR FACING HIS BELOVED FRIEND –
– AND LANCELOT FACING THE MAN WHO HAD BEEN A SECOND FATHER TO HIM.
THE BEST MAN WOULD WIN. THE LOSER WOULD AGREE TO THE WINNER'S TERMS.
MY KING, DO YOU YIELD?
I ASK AGAIN, DO YOU YIELD?
DO WHAT YOU MUST.
NO, YOU WON'T KILL HIM!
NOR WILL ***YOU*** HARM SIR LANCELOT!

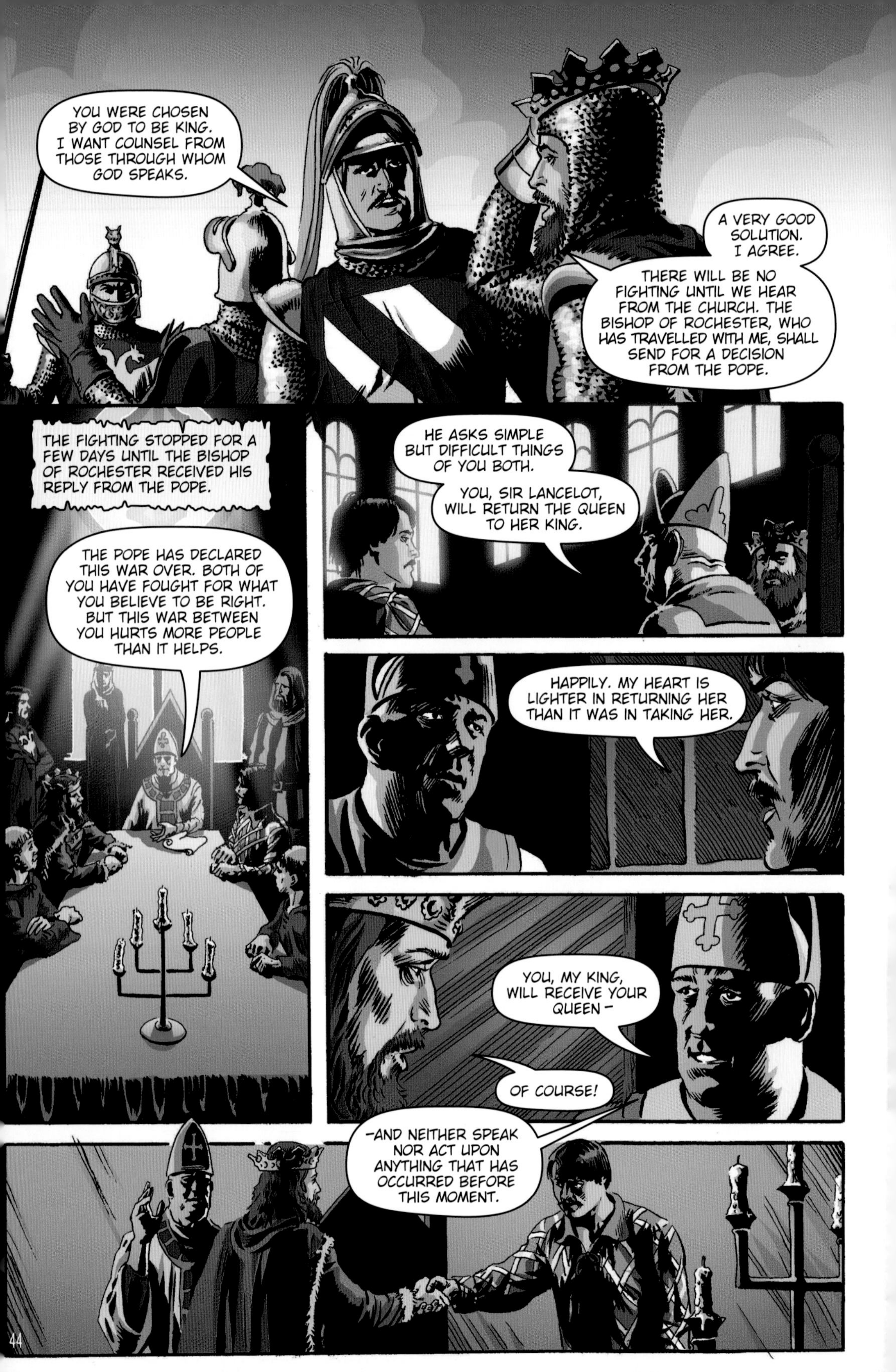
YOU WERE CHOSEN BY GOD TO BE KING. I WANT COUNSEL FROM THOSE THROUGH WHOM GOD SPEAKS.
A VERY GOOD SOLUTION. I AGREE.
THERE WILL BE NO FIGHTING UNTIL WE HEAR FROM THE CHURCH. THE BISHOP OF ROCHESTER, WHO HAS TRAVELLED WITH ME, SHALL SEND FOR A DECISION FROM THE POPE.
THE FIGHTING STOPPED FOR A FEW DAYS UNTIL THE BISHOP OF ROCHESTER RECEIVED HIS REPLY FROM THE POPE.
THE POPE HAS DECLARED THIS WAR OVER. BOTH OF YOU HAVE FOUGHT FOR WHAT YOU BELIEVE TO BE RIGHT. BUT THIS WAR BETWEEN YOU HURTS MORE PEOPLE THAN IT HELPS.
HE ASKS SIMPLE BUT DIFFICULT THINGS OF YOU BOTH.
YOU, SIR LANCELOT, WILL RETURN THE QUEEN TO HER KING.
HAPPILY. MY HEART IS LIGHTER IN RETURNING HER THAN IT WAS IN TAKING HER.
YOU, MY KING, WILL RECEIVE YOUR QUEEN—
OF COURSE!
—AND NEITHER SPEAK NOR ACT UPON ANYTHING THAT HAS OCCURRED BEFORE THIS MOMENT.

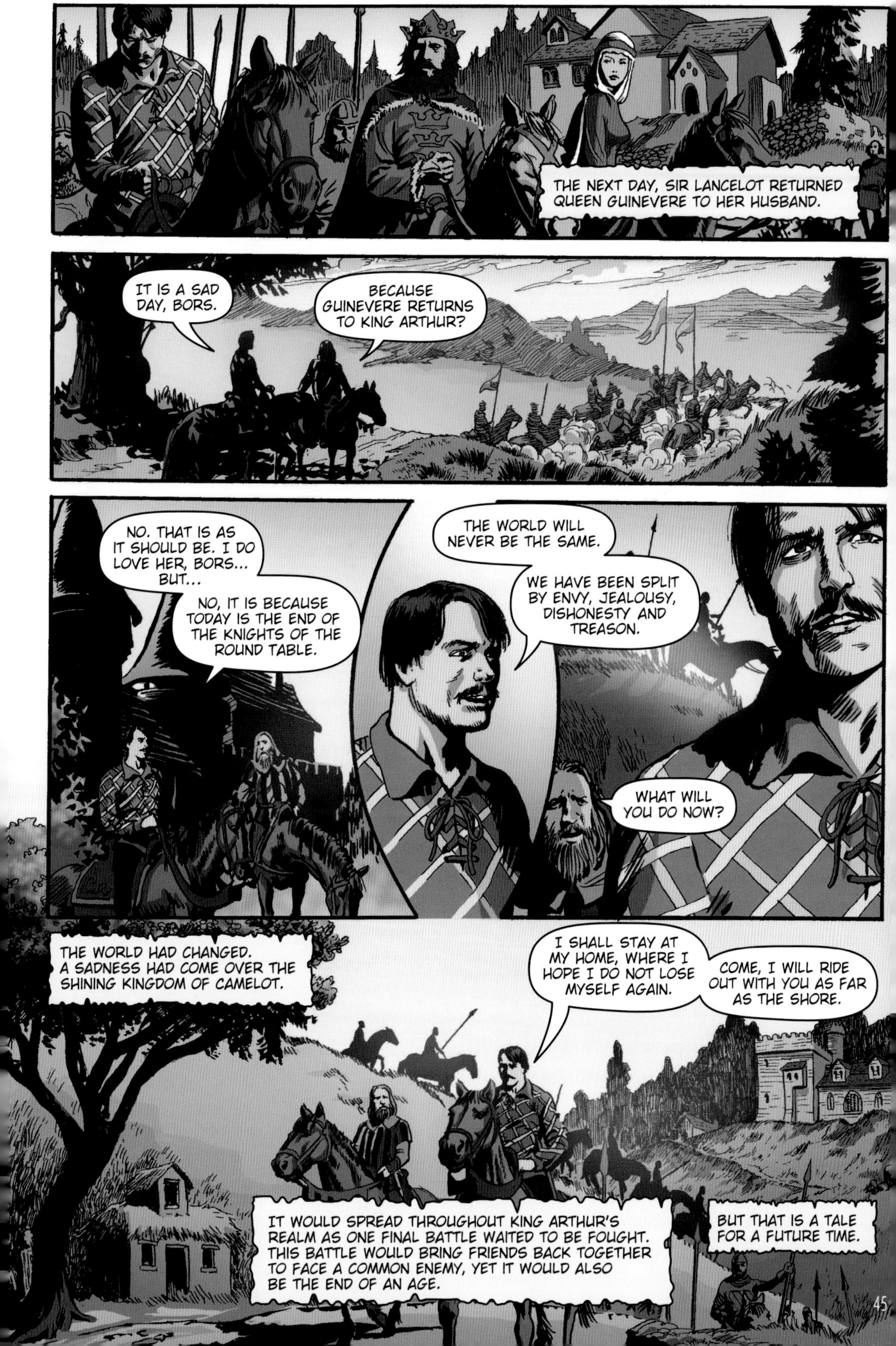
THE NEXT DAY, SIR LANCELOT RETURNED QUEEN GUINEVERE TO HER HUSBAND.
IT IS A SAD DAY, BORS.
BECAUSE GUINEVERE RETURNS TO KING ARTHUR?
NO. THAT IS AS IT SHOULD BE. I DO LOVE HER, BORS... BUT...
NO, IT IS BECAUSE TODAY IS THE END OF THE KNIGHTS OF THE ROUND TABLE.
THE WORLD WILL NEVER BE THE SAME.
WE HAVE BEEN SPLIT BY ENVY, JEALOUSY, DISHONESTY AND TREASON.
WHAT WILL YOU DO NOW?
THE WORLD HAD CHANGED. A SADNESS HAD COME OVER THE SHINING KINGDOM OF CAMELOT.
I SHALL STAY AT MY HOME, WHERE I HOPE I DO NOT LOSE MYSELF AGAIN.
COME, I WILL RIDE OUT WITH YOU AS FAR AS THE SHORE.
IT WOULD SPREAD THROUGHOUT KING ARTHUR'S REALM AS ONE FINAL BATTLE WAITED TO BE FOUGHT. THIS BATTLE WOULD BRING FRIENDS BACK TOGETHER TO FACE A COMMON ENEMY, YET IT WOULD ALSO BE THE END OF AN AGE.
BUT THAT IS A TALE FOR A FUTURE TIME.

GLOSSARY

ARMOUR: metal pieces once worn by soldiers to protect them from knife and arrow wounds

BOON: a favour given in answer to a request

CAMELOT: a castle and surrounding town that served as the capital of Arthur's kingdom

CHIVALRY: a code of behaviour upheld by knights in the Middle Ages. Chivalrous knights vowed to obey religious law, defend the weak, serve their king and protect their country.

COLOURS: specific colours worn by knights and nobility in tournaments and battles. In chivalric tournaments, ladies also gave their colours to favoured knights as a token of admiration.

GAWAIN: one of the Knights of the Round Table

GUINEVERE: King Arthur's wife

HELM: a metal helmet worn with armour. Helms usually had a facepiece that could be moved up and down.

JOUST: a battle on horseback between two knights or among a group of knights. Jousts were often mock battles fought in tournaments. The purpose was merely to knock an opponent out of the saddle, but tournament jousts often resulted in real injuries.

KNIGHT: a mounted soldier sworn to loyally serve a lord or ruler

LANCELOT: a French nobleman and one of the Knights of the Round Table

LIEGE: a superior, such as a lord or king, to whom others owe loyalty

LORD: a ruler or landowner with authority over a group of people

ROUND TABLE: a table given to King Arthur by his father-in-law, Leodegrance. Arthur's greatest knights were all given sieges, or special seats, at the Round Table.

SECOND: a knight or other combatant who assists someone in a one-on-one battle

TOURNAMENT: a series of jousts or sporting battles fought at one time and place

TRIAL BY MIGHT: a one-on-one battle used to settle disputes, also called a trial by combat. In the days before Britain had a regular court system, there were few ways of trying people accused of breaking the law or injuring someone else's rights. To settle certain issues, kings and local rulers allowed trials by might among anyone allowed to bear arms (that is, knights and nobility).

FURTHER READING AND WEBSITES

Camelot Village: Britain's Heritage and History
http://www.camelotintl.com/legend/index.html
This website provides basic information on Arthurian legends, with links to
specific characters and to information on life in medieval England.

Firth, Rachel. *Knights* (Usborne Discovery) Usborne Publishing Ltd., 2008.
Learn more about how people became knights, what weapons they used and how
they defended themselves in battle.

King Arthur and the Knights of the Round Table
http://www.kingarthursknights.com
This website provides articles on the historical and legendary Arthur, a map
and information on Arthurian sites, artwork and the stories of the knights and
other characters of the famous legend.

Limke, Jeff. *King Arthur: Excalibur Unsheathed* Illustrated by Thomas Yeates.
London: Graphic Universe, 2008. This graphic novel begins as young Arthur
pulls a mysterious sword from a stone and finds himself, at the age of ten,
crowned the king of England. The magician Merlin guides Arthur in his
efforts to win peace for his realm.

Morpurgo, Michael. *Arthur High King of Britain* Egmont Books Ltd., 2008.
This wonderfully illustrated book tells the story of how a young boy comes to
be rescued by King Arthur who then tells him the incredible story of his life.
Beginning with the legendary pulling of the sword from the stone to the
eventual fall of Camelot.

CREATING *ARTHUR & LANCELOT: THE FIGHT FOR CAMELOT*

In creating the story, author Jeff Limke adapted *Le Morte d'Arthur*, written
about 1485 by Sir Thomas Malory, an English knight. Artist Thomas Yeates
used historical and traditional sources to shape the story's visual
details. Consultant Andrew Scheil used his knowledge of
Arthurian lore and medieval culture to ensure accuracy.

original pencil from page 22

INDEX

ABOUT THE AUTHOR AND THE ARTIST

JEFF LIMKE was raised in North Dakota, USA, where he first read, listened to and marvelled at Arthurian tales of knights and their adventures. Limke later taught these stories for many years and has written several adaptations of them. His Graphic Myths and Legends work includes *King Arthur: Excalibur Unsheathed, Isis & Osiris: To the Ends of the Earth, Thor & Loki: In the Land of Giants, Jason: Quest for the Golden Fleece* and *Theseus: Battling the Minotaur.*

THOMAS YEATES began his art training in high school and continued at Utah State University and Sacramento State, USA. Yeates has worked as an illustrator for DC Comics, Marvel, Dark Horse and many other companies, drawing Tarzan, Zorro, the Swamp Thing, Timespirits, Captain America and Conan. For Graphic Myths and Legends, he has illustrated *King Arthur: Excalibur Unsheathed, Robin Hood: Outlaw of Sherwood Forest, Atalanta: Race Against Destiny,* and *Odysseus: Escaping Poseidon's Curse.* Yeates lives in northern California, USA with his wife and daughter.

First published in the United States of America in 2008
Copyright © 2008 by Lerner Publishing Group, Inc.